"Ke
"It

Please . . ."

He laughed, a bitter, hollow sound. "Really, it's all too absurd," he said. "It's *you* who are supposed to be guarding *me*. But *I* go running after you like some concerned schoolboy."

"Please, Ken, don't," Sandy pleaded, stepping forward. "It's all just a mistake . . ."

The ship's sudden, shuddery lurch caught Sandy by surprise. Caught off balance, she was thrown forward. She smashed up against his chest, her surprised face just inches from his own. His strong arms went around her waist. His terry bathrobe fell open, and her taut breasts pushed against his bare chest.

She was excruciatingly aware that her wet, flimsy chemise was the only thing keeping her skin from touching his and that his open robe and baggy pajama bottoms left him as nearly naked as she. She could sense his rising passion.

His response was as instantaneous as it was forceful. His mouth strained against hers, his tongue probing greedily. As the great ship plunged ahead through the rough seas, they held each other, swaying together in a delirium of delight . . .

Dear Reader:

As the months go by, we continue to receive word from you that SECOND CHANCE AT LOVE romances are providing you with the kind of romantic entertainment you're looking for. In your letters you've voiced enthusiastic support for SECOND CHANCE AT LOVE, you've shared your thoughts on how personally meaningful the books are, and you've suggested ideas and changes for future books. Although we can't always reply to your letters as quickly as we'd like, please be assured that we appreciate your comments. Your thoughts are all-important to us!

We're glad many of you have come to associate SECOND CHANCE AT LOVE books with our butterfly trademark. We think the butterfly is a perfect symbol of the reaffirmation of life and thrilling new love that SECOND CHANCE AT LOVE heroines and heroes find together in each story. We hope you keep asking for the "butterfly books," and that, when you buy one—whether by a favorite author or a talented new writer—you're sure of a good read. You can trust all SECOND CHANCE AT LOVE books to live up to the high standards of romantic fiction you've come to expect.

So happy reading, and keep your letters coming!

With warm wishes,

Ellen Edwards

Ellen Edwards
SECOND CHANCE AT LOVE
The Berkley/Jove Publishing Group
200 Madison Avenue
New York, NY 10016

Second Chance at Love

GUARDED MOMENTS
LYNN FAIRFAX

A
SECOND CHANCE AT LOVE
BOOK

GUARDED MOMENTS

1

"ALERTNESS, I SUPPOSE that's the first principle," Sandy O'Hara said thoughtfully, glancing down at her bare feet and wiggling her toes. Looking back up at the sea of intent young faces before her, she shook her shoulder-length, straw-blond hair from side to side. The perspiration-dampened tips of her shag-cut fell into place just above her high cheekbones and stayed well away from her large, twinkling blue eyes. She tugged at the hem of her short white jacket and adjusted her belt, then let her arms fall loosely to her sides. She took a deep, relaxing breath, rocked back ever so slightly on her heels, and smiled a gleaming, all-American smile.

The approach of the huge, black-clad man was so swift and unexpected that many people in the audience gasped in surprise.

In one long lunge he was directly behind her. His two outstretched hands clamped brutally around the thin wrist of her right hand and twisted hard.

Instead of trying to pull away from her attacker, Sandy did the unexpected. She stepped toward her assailant with her left foot and at the same time brought her free hand up in a lightning fast back-fist strike against the side of his face.

Surprised, the attacker released his grip, but he was too late. Within seconds he went down under a rain of sharp blows and kicks.

The Georgetown University auditorium shook with the applause and cheers of the students filling it.

Sandy helped her six-and-a-half-foot tall sparring partner, Gus Flowers, up. The hulking giant of a man towered more than a foot over Sandy, but mutual respect was apparent as they stood facing each other and bowed in the fashion of the ancient ritual.

"Any other questions?" Sandy asked with a grin, as she turned to the audience again.

"What if someone grabs your shoulder bag?" a coed in the back called out.

"What if he's got a weapon—a club or something. Is it better to run or what?" asked another.

"And what if someone pins your arms or grabs you around the neck?" asked another concerned young woman.

Dutifully, Sandy and Gus answered all the questions and went through their well-practiced paces. Sandy discussed the latest research findings, gave out hints on how to avoid victim-like behavior, and demonstrated a number of self-defense techniques for every circumstance. Time and again Gus came menacingly at Sandy, and time and again he wound up on the floor. The students roared with delight.

Sandy had known the questions at this lecture would be more pointed and less decorous than at other lectures as the audience contained college students, both male and female, rather than the usual middle-aged ladies of social clubs or P.T.A. groups. Still, it didn't make it any easier when the questions turned personal and she was forced to recall the painful recent past.

"How'd a great-lookin' lady like you get into a racket like this?" a smirking young man in a letter jacket, who was slouched in a front seat, wanted to know.

"My looks had nothing to do with it," Sandy retorted quickly, with a dismissive shrug. "But if you want to know about my background in personal protection, I guess the answer is that it just came naturally to someone like me. I was the only girl in a large family of Irish cops—four generations with the force in Boston."

Hoping to forestall further personal questions, Sandy elaborated lightly, "You can imagine why I came down here for law school with *that* kind of upbringing. But after a couple of years, I decided the practice of law wasn't for me, so I followed my inclinations and joined the Secret Service. They taught me most of what I know about self-defense. After about four years, I went over to the Executive Protection Agency, the big private outfit in McLean. I've been with them for . . . for nearly a year, and, to make a long story short, here I am."

From way in the back another male voice called out loudly to general laughter, "How about a date tonight? You can show me some of those fancy moves."

Sandy allowed herself an amused grin. "I don't really think we have the same moves in mind. Besides, it would be like going out with one of my younger brothers."

She waited for the raucous laughter to subside before saying, "Just one last question, okay? We've already gone over our time limit."

Hoping that this last question would return the audience's attention to the subject of self-defense, Sandy pointed to an earnest-looking coed a few rows back, who was waving her hand vigorously. But this time, Sandy, who was usually a good judge of temperaments, had guessed wrong.

The young woman stood right up, without the slightest hesitation, and asked caustically why Sandy hadn't bothered to stay with the Service when that was just the kind of prestigious position so many other young women were striving so hard and, in too many cases, so fruitlessly to achieve.

And then the memories came back, as strong and disturbing as ever. With a slight tremor in her voice, Sandy began to reply, "For . . . personal reasons, I'm afraid. You see, my husband and I went into the Service together and—and . . . when he was killed I—I just couldn't . . ."

The silence in the auditorium was total. Every face

was riveted to her by the realization that her forthright attempt to answer the innocently probing question was suddenly costing her both poise and self-control.

With her face much redder than it had been during the physical exertions and her huge eyes brimming with tears, Sandy took a deep breath, which she hoped would calm her roiling spirit. But it was no use. Something about the young coed's sincerity and idealism reminded her of herself at that age and brought back all the hopes and dreams senselessly dashed by the accident that had taken his life.

"I'm sorry," Sandy said under her breath to the anticipatory silence. Quickly, she gave a terse little bow. "Excuse me." She turned toward her massive, black-pajama-clad partner. "Please finish up, Gus," she said, an imploring note in her strained voice. Then, without another word, she ran off the stage.

Sandy showered, blow-dried her flaxen hair, and slipped into her shapeless lime-green sweat shirt, matching warm-up pants, and battered track shoes.

It occurred to her fleetingly that, in the days when she and Philly were part of the Secret Service, she would not have gone to receive a new assignment dressed like this. In the last year, she had paid little attention to her wardrobe or appearance. She supposed she had been living in the past to an unhealthy degree, and she knew that, in spite of her tears just now—embarrassingly public tears—her period of mourning was about to end.

A steaming hot shower and half an hour alone in the locker room were all she needed to regain her composure and revive her spirits.

She picked up her canvas carry-all bag and her gray parka and stepped into the hallway, where kind-hearted, hatchet-faced Gus was waiting for her.

The pug-ugly, one-time FBI agent reached down and gave her shoulder a consoling pat. "Those kids didn't know," he growled in his gravelly voice, "but don't you worry about nothin', Sandy. I took care of it for you. I told 'em just what you were fixin' to say about the huntin' accident on the Eastern shore and how you was sweethearts way back to school days, and how you just couldn't take it workin' longside all his old friends in the Service—the same people that were there that day and all. Hell, the kids understood. They know these things happen sometimes. It was okay."

"Thanks, Gus," Sandy said gratefully, as they began to walk slowly out to the parking lot. "I know I shouldn't get upset like that. After all, it's been a year already . . ."

"These things happen sometimes," Gus repeated in a gruff grumble that couldn't entirely disguise the tender sentiment underneath it.

When they stepped out into the cold, crisp air of the January winter day, Sandy stopped to put on her parka. From one pocket she took out a pair of fur-lined, black-leather gloves. From the other she pulled a dark-blue wool stocking cap.

Before making his way over to his battered Chevy, Gus walked her to the bike racks and waited while she unlocked the canary-yellow racing bike, a super-light-weight twelve-speed that Sandy rode everywhere in Washington, partly because it was economical, but mostly because it helped keep her in shape. He watched patiently while she strapped her bag to the back of the bike. Then she zipped up the parka, pulled on her gloves, tugged the cap down over her ears, and hopped onto the bicycle.

Gus looked bashfully down at the snow-covered road. "Be careful now, ridin' that thing through the streets," he mumbled, his breath coming out in icy puffs.

"Okay, Gus," Sandy said softly. "I will. And you take care, too, okay? I'll be back in touch as soon as I can." She leaned over from her perch on the bicycle and kissed the red-faced old giant on the side of his face. "I'll miss you, Gus," she said, starting to pedal away.

"I'll miss you too," Gus muttered without looking up. As she rode off, he called out after her, "If you don't like this new assignment of yours, you come on back, you hear? Don't forget now! You come on back any-time..."

"I will, Gus, I will," she shouted back, taking a hand off the handlebars just long enough to wave. Then she bumped down over the low curb and coasted out into the empty street. Soon she had rounded the corner and was on her way across town to Capitol Hill, the unlikely place where she was to receive her marching orders.

She would miss Gus and the pleasant routine of their daily workout demonstrations. But, after nearly a year of this routine combined with self-imposed seclusion, she felt ready to venture out into this new phase of her life.

Sandy was familiar with most of the miles of bike paths in and around central Washington, and she enjoyed pedaling along them in every season of the year. It didn't take her long to make her way through the quiet town-house-lined streets of Georgetown, down along ice-bound Rock Creek, over to snow-covered Potomac Park and across the tree-lined Mall to the U.S. Capitol.

Still, she was late. Sandy parked hurriedly, and locked her bicycle, ran up the broad front stairs of the Capitol, and dashed inside. She found herself standing under the imposing Rotunda dome, not far from a small group of tourists, before she realized that she didn't have the slightest idea where in the Capitol complex she was sup-posed to go.

The Hill was an odd choice for this meeting anyway, Sandy thought as she pulled off her gloves and fumbled around in the pockets of her parka for the slip of paper on which she'd scribbled the room number.

But then again, everything about the assignment had been out of the ordinary, she reminded herself as she idly watched the tourists, a small group of middle-aged

people, with their backs to her. They had arranged themselves for a photograph with a tall, distinguished-looking
man in a dark, well-tailored suit. Even though he had
his back to her, Sandy could tell from his ramrod-straight
posture, the sharp razor-cut of his black hair, and the
excited way the women in the group pushed against each
other to be as close to him as possible, that he had to be
one of the charismatic "Princes of the Hill."

Sandy watched the photographer, a portly middle-
aged man in a red plaid jacket, who was obviously part
of the tourist group, waving and gesturing as he looked
through the camera to make certain all the women were
inside the frame of the picture. She dug into her pockets,
thinking how unexpected it had been to get the word for
this meeting straight from the highest echelons of the
Secret Service, from her former boss in fact, instead of
through the usual channels in the McLean office.

Where *was* that slip of paper? She never used to be
this careless. It certainly was time to get back in the
groove. Frustrated with herself, she swore under her
breath, reached up, pulled off her stocking cap and shook
out her blond hair.

Instantly, two things happened. First, when she looked
down at the blue wool cap in her hand, she found the
crumpled paper that had been inside it all along. Simultaneously, from the corner of her eye, she saw the camera
that the plaid-jacketed man was looking into veer wildly
toward her and away from the tourists and the tall man
posed in their midst.

The man with the camera looked up and gawked at
her. Then, ignoring both the tall Congressional Prince
and the startled ladies surrounding him, he ran right past
them—his hurried footsteps echoing in the vast space of
the Rotunda—straight over to Sandy.

"Jiminy!" he expostulated, awe in his voice and wonder in his eyes. "What're *you* doin' *here*? I seen *all* your
pictures 'cept that jungle one 'cause my wife said it was

porno-ographic . . ." His excited voice trailed off. Squinting closely at her, he did a shocked doubletake. "Oh, jiminy, I *am* sorry," he apologized. As he realized his mistake, his ruddy face turned even redder with embarrassment.

"It's okay," Sandy mumbled, wondering to herself if it would help to start wearing sunglasses around town. This sort of thing had been happening ever more frequently since that day, several months after Philly's death, when she had allowed her new hairdresser to convince her to get rid of the prim bouffant hairstyle she had been wearing since the eighth grade in favor of her present ultra-modern shag.

"Nobody's worn the Prom Queen look since Eisenhower!" her hairdresser had reproved peevishly, his hands on his slim hips. "And nobody with that skin of yours should wear all that make-up either!" She had taken his advice, and he had turned out to be spectacularly right. Men had always been interested in her, but now they seemed attracted in droves. The political wives she was usually assigned to guard began complaining. And eventually the word came down—her important female charges weren't interested in being upstaged by their own bodyguard. Her boss at the Executive Protection Agency had had no choice but to assign her to the martial arts demonstrations. Eventually Sandy had gotten used to the attention her new look brought, but sometimes it was annoying nonetheless.

Behind the embarrassed tourist, one of the women called out in an exasperated tone, "Harold, you come back here this instant! Can't you see you're keeping the Senator waiting?"

Sandy looked past discomfited Harold to the Senator, who had turned slightly and was giving her a cool, appraising look over his broad, well-tailored shoulder. She knew he looked vaguely familiar from what she could see of him, but she couldn't quite place him.

Sandy had no great need to identify every celebrity she passed in a day around Washington. Like many people in her business, she was both more blasé about and less familiar with the nationally known political figures in the city than the average tourist. This particular senator *was* quite handsome, she noted as she automatically adopted the slightly superior attitude toward politicians that she had learned from her father and brothers, who had guarded many a Boston politico in their times. "Didn't I see his picture in the paper recently?" Sandy asked absentmindedly.

"Yes, indeed, miss," Harold told her. He was about to elaborate when a thin, blondish man in a brown suit appeared at his side, seemingly out of nowhere.

Nodding perfunctorily at Sandy, the man whispered hoarsely in Harold's ear, "I'm afraid the Senator is late for his appointments as it is, sir. So if you would be kind enough to come along with me, please . . ." Deftly, he took the still transfixed Harold by the elbow and steered him away.

Harold was escorted back by the man who, Sandy was certain, was one of the Senator's aides. As Harold reached the center of the Rotunda, he peered back over his shoulder and yelled out, so loudly that everyone else in the cavernous hall was able to hear, "As far as I'm concerned, little lady, you're a 'ten' anyway! Yes, indeed!"

An amused, sophisticated expression flickered across the Senator's dark, aristocratically handsome features. Instinctively, Sandy looked away, never having gotten a full, front view of his face. Then she gasped, noticing the crumpled slip of paper still in her hand and realizing she was late for her appointment. Without another glance in the Senator's direction, she turned and ran out of the Rotunda, hoping she was going in the right direction.

2

MINUTES LATER, SANDY stood at the end of the richly gleaming hallway in the Senate wing, absolutely at a loss. Where to turn next? *Why* hadn't she taken the time a moment ago to write down the security guard's directions? she moaned to herself.

"A right, then a left, then another right. It's at the end of the hall there. You can't miss it," the friendly uniformed guard had assured her. But here she was— late, lost, and the room number she was looking for was nowhere in sight! From this moment forward, she vowed to herself, she was going to regain the efficiency of the old Sandy O'Hara.

She sighed, pausing a moment to gather her wits, taking the time to admire the intricately detailed Brumidi frescoes that covered the vaulted ceiling and the pale amber walls and the shining glazed tiles that reflected the soft golden light.

Then she marched up to the blank, unnumbered door at the end of the hall. She put her hand on the knob and took a deep breath. *If* she remembered the guard's instructions correctly, *then* this was the right room. If not . . .

She turned the handle decisively, pulled open the unmarked door, and . . .

"Oh, no!" Sandy groaned, rolling her eyes heavenward so she wouldn't have to look at the array of neatly stacked brooms and buckets and the shelves of cleansers and waxes in the broom closet before her. "Oh, no," she repeated, not really hearing the rapid tattoo of footsteps approaching from just around the corner.

Still holding onto the open door of the broom closet, as if for support, she stepped back a pace and collided with the large solid, masculine body of someone who had come racing around the corner.

"Oof!" The sharp impact knocked the air out of her lungs, and she almost slipped on the highly waxed floor, but the man caught her in his arms. As he held her, she could feel him looking about quickly, anxiously scanning the corner around which he'd just come. His decisive glances instantly took in the open door, the broom closet, then fell on Sandy herself.

As she regained her balance, she had just enough time to glimpse the hooded dark eyes, the aquiline nose, the full head of black hair streaked with strands of premature gray at the temples and to realize that this was the same man—the handsome Senator—whom she had just seen in the Capitol Rotunda.

And she had just enough time to decide that this tall, darkly handsome, charismatic public figure was *somehow* being pursued when, without a word, he stepped forward, pulled her with him into the closet, and closed the door after them. Abruptly they were thrown into complete darkness.

"What the—" she began, but he quickly put his hand over her mouth.

"Shhh!" he whispered urgently. "They're right outside!"

She was about to demand an explanation, demand to be released *instantly*—or else!—when she heard the tiny scrabbling sounds and deep, muffled voices just on the other side of the door.

Feeling the Senator's strong arms around her waist and the little flutters of his breath on her face, Sandy braced herself for the unexpected. But she was totally unprepared for what happened next.

In the blackness of the broom closet, the Senator pulled

her close to him and kissed her—long, hard and passionately on the lips!

She didn't struggle; she didn't squirm; she didn't try to fight free of the Senator's determined lips so she could protest or cry out for help. Instead, her response was automatic, honed by long months of rigorous training.

She "followed through," matching and complementing the Senator's movements with similar movements of her own. Rather than pulling away, she pushed even closer, until her hips were grinding against his and her breasts were in full contact with his powerful chest. Her pinioned arms slipped around his waist, her hands clasping together behind the small of his back. She pulled him still closer to her, meeting the pressure of his muscular body with her own. And with that, she had won the "inside" position, those few millimeters of space that were all she needed to launch a debilitating counterattack.

But something strange was happening. She didn't know his intention or even his name, though she felt that if she could get a good look at him for *long* enough, his name would probably come to her. At this moment, the exalted Senator was kissing her so forcefully in the dark of this Capitol Hill broom closet that her awareness was narrowing to the more intimate details of his body—how strong and fit he felt, how muscular his chest was, how trim and narrow his waist.

There was increasing urgency in the way his stroking hands swirled around her back. She could feel his rising passion, and her eyes fluttered closed in a rapture of delight. A new wind was rising in the long calm center of her heart.

Suddenly the Senator pulled away from her and, holding her shoulders in his powerful hands, he cocked his head toward the hall outside. Sandy heard nothing but the thudding of her own heart. Whoever had been pursuing this bold and obviously self-assured politician had vanished among the labyrinthine corridors of Capitol Hill.

What bit of national scandal she might have just played a role in, Sandy couldn't guess. Obviously, she had been useful to the Senator there holding the closet door open, offering him a hiding place at just the right moment. But why had he kissed her? Why was he still holding her against his tall, hard frame, which smelled—now she recognized the sweet, lemony odor—overwhelmingly of Murphy's Oil Soap?

He held her away from him, and this time turned toward the door. Slowly he turned the handle and a slant of bright light fell on his shoulder as he looked gingerly around the door jamb.

"All clear," he whispered back to Sandy. Stepping into the closet again, he said, "I guess I was saved by a—Number Ten!"

Sandy could think of no response. She simply stood there, wishing she could see him better. It hardly seemed appropriate at this point to ask, "But who *are* you?" And, in any case, it was coming to her.

But before she had made any more progress through her confusion, the Senator leaned over and placed a gentle kiss on her forehead. "Thank you," he said, giving her a long conspiratorial wink and then making a swift exit, leaving the door slightly ajar.

Sandy just stood there flabbergasted and staring after him, wondering what had just happened to her. Then she felt angry. What on earth did this man take her for? Never mind who *he* was. Who did he think *she* was? What right had he—closed in a closet or not—to kiss a total stranger? She was beginning to steam with rage when she suddenly realized that all thoughts of her meeting and its still unknown location had been chased away from her mind by the bizarre events of the last couple of minutes.

Quickly she raced back down the hallway, retracing her steps to the Rotunda, and started to search for the room again. As she ran, Sandy vowed to herself that this time she would pay better attention to where she was going. But her concentration was clouded by the vivid memory of the salty taste of the handsome Senator's lips and the disturbing feel of his hard body pressing against hers. Once again she took a wrong turn.

Ten more precious minutes elapsed before she finally found the right room. By then Sandy was more than a half hour late.

She burst through the door, apologizing profusely for being late. Fortunately, the friendly, efficient-looking secretary in the nondescript anteroom offered her a chair and assured her that it didn't matter in the slightest because Mr. Milner—who was Sandy's former boss in the Secret Service—was still with his earlier appointment. He wasn't quite ready to see her yet anyway.

Sandy barely had time to catch her breath before her attention was drawn to an angry bellow coming from the other side of the thin partition separating the anteroom from the interior office. The voice was so loud and clear that it was impossible not to listen, or to realize that the harshly truculent words were about her.

She could tell that these hoarse phrases, spoken in a rapid Irish-accented lilt, belonged to her former boss's visitor: "Didn't you give a thought at all to what you were doin', man? Are you tryin' t' ruin us? When we asked you for a security man who would not stand out like some thug in a crowd of society swells, did you have to go to the other extreme? Did you have to send us a lass, man?"

She immediately recognized her one-time Secret Service boss's tired, but sweetly reasonable voice replying, "Come now, Fitz, calm down. No one's trying to do your people in. I don't think you're aware of the complete picture here. First off, look at her qualifications—those expert marksman scores, the double black belts. Then, most importantly, consider *this*," he added, his voice lowering to a buzzing whisper that Sandy couldn't decipher.

Unintentionally straining forward to hear more, Sandy found herself the object of the secretary's sympathetic expression. "Don't worry about a thing, dear," the secretary said in a confidential whisper. "I'm sure Mr. Milner is going to take care of *everything.*"

"Oh yes, I'm sure he will," Sandy agreed glumly, wishing she knew what Foster Milner and the unknown man with the Irish accent were saying to each other now.

"Listen, dear," the secretary continued, "you know this assignment is the envy of the Service, don't you?" She hooked a long-nailed finger over her shoulder, pointing to the inside office. "That's Fitzpatrick Kenneally in there with Mr. Milner. He's Rexford's chief aide, and he's definitely full of bluster, but I wouldn't worry about what he says if I were you. I'm certain Mr. Milner wouldn't make a move unless he knew Ken Rexford would approve."

"Ken Rexford?" Sandy repeated hesitantly.

"Uh-huh," the secretary said enthusiastically. "Ken Rexford. You're going to be the bodyguard—the *only* bodyguard, as far as I know—on a three-month, 'round-the-world, luxury-liner cruise with Ken Rexford, the former Senator from California. And *what* a body that is to be guarding! I mean, not only is there talk he might someday run for President, not only is he one of the most eligible bachelors in the country, if not in the entire world, but he's absolutely filthy rich besides! Honey, if I only had three months alone with Senator Rexford . . ."

Senator Rexford! At last the right name came together with the face, *that* face, in Sandy's mind. That's who he was! He was the Senator—or rather, former Senator—from California who had astounded everyone at the end of the summer by suddenly pulling out of the race against some veteran politician for his own practically assured Senate seat. There had been talk; some sort of scandal? Sandy couldn't remember, but her whole face was turning scarlet with embarrassment.

The secretary gave her a peculiar look. "You okay, dear?" she asked. But before Sandy could reply, the secretary went on, "Oh, they might have used the regular Secret Service for this trip, even though the Senator is technically a private citizen. But what with that little war going on on that island of Mauristan and everything, the Service is being heavily leaned on—the Secretary of State's trips trying to negotiate peace and all.

"Mr. Milner has had an office over here for a few days to help Senator Rexford plan his trip. I guess protection through a private agency seemed the easiest to arrange. The trip came up kind of suddenly, I guess."

The secretary was obviously a good source of information, but before Sandy had had time to digest her words, the door to the inner sanctum flew open and not *one*, but *two*, familiar figures appeared. She had already seen the man in the rumpled brown suit that white-haired Foster Milner was escorting out of the office! He was the man who had dragged Harold, the ardent tourist, away from her in the Rotunda less than an hour ago!

Noticing her sitting in the chair, her old boss led the light-haired senatorial aide over to her. "I'm glad you're here," Foster began good-naturedly. "Sandy O'Hara, I want you to meet Fitzpatrick Kenneally, chief legislative aide to former Senator Rexford of California."

As Sandy rose from her chair, Senator Rexford's chief legislative aide extended his hand and forced a reluctant, professional smile to his face.

"Hello, Miss O'Hara," he began, stopping suddenly as soon as he had taken one good look at her. His mouth fell open, and his hand dropped back to his side. *"You!"* he gasped. "Saints preserve us, it's *you!*"

"Oh, do you two know each other?" Sandy's old boss asked innocently.

"Know each other?" Fitzpatrick Kenneally sputtered. "Good lord, man, you could have told me she was such a beauty besides!" Fixing Sandy with a steely, suspicious glare, he asked abruptly, "Why do you use the name 'Sandy' on your personnel records and not 'Sandra'? *That's* what caused all the confusion for us, lass."

She shrugged. "Sandra isn't my name, I'm afraid," she replied apologetically. "You see, we have all boys in my family, and my father had already named my older brother Alexander and Sandra is a variation of Alexandra, as I'm sure you know. So, to avoid confusion, he named me Sandy. It's right on my birth certificate like that— Sandy O'Hara. I'm sorry if it caused you any trouble but . . ."

Kenneally threw up his hands. "Stop, woman, stop!" Shaking his head, he muttered, "To avoid confusion, indeed!" He turned and walked to the door. "I'll be talking to the Senator about this," he said over his shoulder as he left.

After the Senator's chief aide had slammed the door shut behind him, Foster Milner put his arm around Sandy's shoulder and led her into his private office, letting a broad grin cross his face after he shut the door.

"Well, Sandy," he said in a near whisper, "I guess when I sent over my recommendation I neglected to point out that you are Ms. Sandy O'Hara." His eyes twinkled with amusement. "The Senator may not go for the idea of a female bodyguard any more than Kenneally does, but you're the most qualified person for the job. Of that, there is no doubt."

He went on to tell her that she would remain on the private Executive Protection Agency's payroll for this assignment, even though the Secret Service was cooperating with them to make arrangements. "The Senator still plays an active role in some domestic and foreign policy matters. He advises various groups and committees, you know," Milner explained. "We keep a protective eye on him from time to time."

Her former boss added that, for now, Sandy's assignment was off the record and that, as always, he relied on her good judgment and discretion in keeping her plans to herself.

He explained that her new job should be quite simple and relaxing. The presence of a bodyguard on Senator Rexford's cruise was mostly a formality. "Just a precaution, Sandy. With public figures these days, you never know. I'm sure you'd be ready to take action if any threat to his safety should arise."

Milner outlined the mouth-watering itinerary—Los Angeles, Hawaii, Pago Pago, another South Seas island she had never heard of, Manila, Hong Kong, Bangkok, Sri Lanka, Bombay, Mahe, Cape Town, Rio, Salvador de Bahia...

He told her that in most of these places Senator Rexford's family had holdings and financial interests, and that it was the purpose of the trip—in addition to being a vacation for the hard-working former senator—to survey the far-flung, worldwide possessions of his family.

Milner added, as an aside, that on certain of their stops there would be ceremonial occasions, as befitted a man of Senator Rexford's eminence. For these events, in particular, when the Senator would be out among the public, Sandy would have to be on high alert. But passengers sailing on the cruise would all have been well screened by Milner's office ahead of time, and Sandy herself would have access to dossiers on their backgrounds. But for the most part, she could consider the cruise something of a vacation.

Since shipboard life was quite formal, Sandy would naturally get quite a hefty clothing allowance to buy "evening gowns and stuff like that." Milner pointed to her shapeless warm-up suit. "Get something more ap-

propriate than a sweatshirt for mingling in high society."
Sandy could feel a warm flush travelling up her cheeks.

"Oh," she said. "That will be nice. I haven't bought
a new evening gown since I left the Secret Service, and
all those elegant politicians' wives..." Milner gave her
an understanding look, which said he knew she hadn't
been up to partying much in the last year.

"You'll need to be in Los Angeles at the end of the
month, ready to board," he concluded, standing up and
signalling that the meeting was over. "We'll take care
of the rest."

"Well..." Sandy stood up. "This *is* on the up-and-
up, Foster?"

"Of course! Don't tell me you've got to think twice
about an opportunity like *this!*" he answered, a tinge of
rebuke in his avuncular voice. He put an arm around
Sandy's shoulders and led her slowly out the door. "I
wouldn't steer you wrong," he assured her. "And anyway," he added, "you can't stay in Washington giving
those self-defense demonstrations all your life. You've
got too much on the ball. Now, I think it's time you put
the past behind you. We both know Philly would've
wanted it that way, too."

"Okay," Sandy said in a small voice. "You're right,
of course. I'll do it."

As she left Foster's, the image of a man's face flashed
across her mind. But for the first time in a year, it wasn't
the face of her deceased husband that haunted her.

It was another face. The complete opposite of the face
of the boy she had grown up with, who had become her
husband. A dark face, while Philly's had been fair.
Amused and sardonic, while Philly's had been earnest.
Worldly, while Philly had been the picture of innocence.

The contrast confused her. She shook her head, as if
to clear her mind. How could she let a face glimpsed
briefly across the crowded Capitol rotunda...a face that

had pressed against hers, taking complete advantage of a most unusual situation . . . a face she had last seen winking at her, as though she were part of some frivolous joke . . . how could she allow such a face to stir up her feelings?

Never, she thought, as she found herself finally outside the massive Capitol building, trotting down its broad white steps. Never, she thought, unlocking the cold metal lock on her bicycle and breathing in the biting winter air.

She might be about to launch herself on a three-month 'round-the-world cruise with that face, with Senator Kenneth Rexford, but she was not going to let feelings that had died with Philly come back into her life now. And certainly not in connection with a flirtatious, flippant playboy like . . . That was what she had read about him! Now it came back to her.

California Senator Drops Out of Race. What had followed that headline? *Fearing his reputation as playboy* and to protect himself from the revelation of certain scandals he was involved in, he had ducked out of the election. His "outside activities" might cost him too many votes. He had decided not to run, to protect his reputation, or what was left of it.

Now Sandy was sure. He was the one who had been dubbed by the press the "Bachelor Senator."

She would treat this assignment like any other, even if he looked on her as his aide Kenneally did—as inadequate protection because she was a woman. He would probably treat her like some temporary Girl Friday, and send her trotting around on all his minor errands. He would probably want her to scout out all the broom closets on the ship, so he would know where to hide at inconvenient moments. He would probably want . . . Sandy shuddered.

If he thought that long kisses in dark places came

along with the protection services of a female bodyguard, former U. S. Senator Kenneth Rexford of California had another think coming.

He might be the Senator. But she was to be his bodyguard. And that would be the extent of their relationship.

3

THE LIMOUSINE APPEARED like a long, black apparition out of the swirling snowstorm.

From where she sat curled up on her blue corduroy couch, sipping tea and reading a paperback mystery, Sandy had a perfect view out the front window of her chilly apartment. She watched with increasing curiosity as a uniformed chauffeur hopped out of the powerful-looking, black Lincoln, wreathed in steam from the exhaust of its idling engine. To her amazement, the chauffeur headed straight for her door and knocked.

"Miss O'Hara?"

"Yes." Sandy stood at the open doorway, eyeing the chauffeur warily.

"The Senator's respects, miss," the chauffeur said, touching the tip of his driver's cap. "Senator Rexford asks that you join him in the car."

"Senator Rexford? Now?"

"Yes'm. If it's convenient."

"I'll be out in a few moments," Sandy said nervously. "Would you like to wait inside?"

"No thank you, miss. It's best if I stay out here where I can keep my eye on the car," the chauffeur replied.

"As you wish," she said, absentmindedly closing the door.

What was *he* doing here? How had he found her address, she wondered, and, catching herself, she realized that, of course, by now his aide would have told him about her assignment. He probably already had a dossier on her.

She scrambled around the bathroom until she found her hairbrush and lipstick. How could she be irritated when, after all, a U. S. Senator—a former one to be sure, but in any case, a major political personage—was waiting outside in a limousine to *see* her?

She looked down at her clothes and was glad she had already started to refurbish her wardrobe. Her new fire-engine red slacks were well cut, and her hand-knit Irish white wool sweater tucked up under her chin in a fashionable cowl. She had no time to change into something less casual. It would do, she thought, and, taking her new down coat out of her bedroom closet, she simultaneously slipped her stockinged feet into a pair of new, medium-heeled black boots. She gave a shake to her shoulder-length mane of shaggy blond hair, took a deep breath, and opened the door.

"Ready," she said brightly to the chauffeur, who was standing in the swirling currents of snowy wind, stamping his feet and slapping his arms against his sides.

"This way, miss," he said through chattering teeth, obviously relieved to be leading her to the warmth of the big car. Already the limousine's windows were fogged over and lightly dusted by the falling snow. The chauffeur opened the rear door, and Sandy stepped inside, into the warmth. The rich leather and polished wood of the luxury automobile's interior seemed to glow even in the dim light.

"Hello again, Ms. O'Hara," former Senator Ken Rexford said in that deep baritone voice of his, gesturing to her to take a seat.

She sat down where he pointed, across from him with her back to the glassed-in partition that divided them from the chauffeur. She was facing him. She was so close that their knees almost touched.

"Hello, Senator Rexford," she said softly, forcing herself to look into his deep, dark eyes.

He took off one of the leather gloves he was wearing and held out his hand. Quickly, Sandy removed a glove and, somewhat awkwardly, shook his hand. How warm his touch was, she thought, barely hearing when he reached forward, pressed a button on a console next to her and said, "Drive slowly around the block, please, Everett."

Sandy's mouth went dry and she found that she was suddenly conscious of the sound of her own breath. The Senator was even handsomer and more refined-looking than she remembered. He looked nothing short of elegant, dressed in a camel-hair topcoat over a dark business suit and wearing a trim alpaca tie.

He leaned back and cast an enigmatic and appraising smile at her. "I am here for two reasons, Ms. O'Hara." he said in businesslike tones. "And I haven't long. I am on my way to the airport."

Outside the windows of the limousine Sandy could see nothing but a flapping curtain of white snow. She wondered if its brightness was causing her dizziness. She breathed deeply and said nothing.

"First of all," he went on, letting his gloved hand fall casually against the back of the leather seat. "About the way in which we met...I want you to know that you saved me from a potentially delicate situation. Since I've been out of office, the press gets curious every time I'm on the Hill to talk to someone, wanting to know what I'm up to. I had no desire to explain to *The New York Times* and *The Washington Post* why I was there that day. I was spared a difficult encounter when I chose to disappear from that corridor. I wanted you to know that, no matter what you may have heard about my reputation, it wasn't simply that I am in the habit of jumping into broom closets with beautiful women."

"Reputation?" Sandy repeated innocently.

The Senator waved his hand, as if searching for the right word. "You know, all that 'womanizer' and 'rich dilettante' business. The papers manage to build whatever picture they want to of a public figure. We are totally at their mercy. It's not true, you know."

"Sure," Sandy said with a shrug, not quite certain what he was getting at. She was thinking of what her father had always said about the necessity of impartiality, of not getting involved in either the personal life or the views of a politician if you had to guard him. "I can forget how we met, if you'd like," she added.

"Yes, well, maybe you should. I really can't explain what happened there in that closet . . ." He smiled a slow, deliberate grin. "I guess I just did what came naturally . . ."

The Senator did not seem to notice that his last remark stood in direct contradiction to his claim that he was not really a born playboy. Though she had a strong urge to point this out, Sandy chose instead to smile demurely and say nothing.

"My second point, Ms. O'Hara, has to do with your appointment as my bodyguard for the trip I am taking to the South Pacific. I cannot pretend that I was not surprised when my aide told me that Mr. Milner had recommended a woman for the job." He let out a little snort with the word "woman" that seemed to sum up his attitude toward the usefulness of the entire sex for anything other than his pleasure. Sandy was beginning to boil inside.

"It *is* unusual, I suppose, Senator," she managed to answer politely. "There are not many women who have gone as far as I have through the training required for executive protection." Somehow she had found the nerve to give him that response and look him straight in the eye at the same time.

"Perhaps not. However, I thought you might wish to reconsider, Ms. O'Hara, while there is still time to replace you. Although this trip is being billed to the public as a pleasure cruise — and for the most part it will be — certain dangers could arise along the way. As you saw the other day, there are those who are anxious to confront me . . . some sensitive issues . . . people I will need to avoid. I am sure you wouldn't want to find yourself in a situation you couldn't handle."

"I rarely do, Senator. And if what you're really saying is that you haven't enough confidence in my abilities to protect you, may I point out that I did quite well the other day, without even knowing that was what I was doing."

As soon as the words were out, Sandy was afraid they had sounded flirtatious, obliquely referring to their closeness in the closet. She took a hasty vow that she would never flirt with this man, even in the most innocent way. He didn't deserve it. His condescending attitude was infuriating.

But before she knew what had happened, the Senator had fixed her with his dark, intense eyes. With a seeming impulsiveness that both surprised and shocked Sandy, he took her in his arms and pressed his mouth against hers.

His strength and his touch came back to her like a wave washing over her. But she pushed against his shoulders, making little sounds of protest, until he released her and, breaking into a wide smile, held her at arm's length.

"I don't recall that you had any problem about kissing me when we met," he said.

"Senator," she said, sitting up straighter and trying her best to seem composed, "from this moment on, I am your bodyguard. My job is to protect you from danger and harm. I would like you to know that I am also quite capable of using various techniques I know to defend *myself*. And if that is necessary, I will. I have no intention of backing away from this job, however much you might wish it."

The big black limousine skidded to a stop on an icy street corner, and the jolt made Sandy aware of the chance for her exit. She put her hand on the door handle. "I'll be in Los Angeles on the day you sail. Until then, Senator, safe journey." She turned the handle, pushed open the door, and jumped out of the car.

He called out after her as she dashed away into the bitter cold of the gray, snowy day. She couldn't tell what he was saying. She didn't want to know. And she didn't want to hear his laughter, if that was what the sound was, now half lost in the wind.

Sandy didn't turn her head or slow her running feet until the black limousine behind her had disappeared behind the falling snow and she was safely back home.

Sandy O'Hara's last martial arts demonstration, in the auditorium at Georgetown University, had taken place on a cold Washington morning in early January. The grand ocean liner, the *Voyager Queen,* would depart the port of Los Angeles on its gloriously luxurious, eighty-nine-day, around-the-world maiden cruise at the end of the same month. During the three weeks she had between assignments, Sandy was far from idle.

She had dossiers to read, itineraries to study. She had to get her shots and her various papers. And she had to use all her old Secret Service connections just to make certain that her renewed passport came back in time.

When she had a chance, she read the newspapers, as part of her effort to start keeping up with what was going on in the world. When she and Philly had been in the Secret Service, between the two of them, they had known everything that went on at home and abroad and could catch every nuance of foreign policy decisions made in Washington. But her interest had slipped away since Philly's death, especially in those things they had shared so closely.

Now, she noted, tensions between the U.S. and Russia seemed to be running high again, sparked by the civil war on the little island of Mauristan, which had been going on since early summer. Sandy had never even heard of it, but there it was on a map in the paper, off the coast of North Africa.

One group of Mauristanians had laid claim to a vast find of oil reserves discovered recently underneath the island, and the Russians seemed to be successfully wooing this faction. The papers said it might be only a matter of time before the Russians saw to it that north Mauristan was in complete control of the island, and thus had total access to the oil.

South Mauristan also claimed the oil reserves and had appealed to the United States to help them keep the oil out of the hands of their northern countrymen and the Soviets. Sandy sighed as she read the day's headlines. American warships had steamed toward Mauristan and Russian planes were reputed to be landing supplies and possibly troops there. The United Nations had called an emergency meeting, but so far all hands were tied and heads locked in the crisis.

Sandy was glad her cruise wasn't going through waters near that brouhaha. She wasn't sure she was ready to take on the tensions of the world after all. She tossed *The Washington Post* on the floor and turned to the enormous stack of papers on the table next to her.

She really didn't have time to read leisurely anyway. There was so much paperwork to be done and so many documents to study before she left for Los Angeles that Sandy was having to force herself to take time for the many shopping expeditions to Washington's chic boutiques that were required to gather up a new wardrobe before her departure.

Luckily, Washington was used to clientele preparing for trips south in the winter and carried a full line of cruise-wear, from bathing suits to long evening gowns. Though in the beginning something in Sandy had resisted working on her new image, little by little she began to enjoy choosing the smart sportswear and designer dresses that would launch her on her new life.

The generous check she had received to help her prepare for the trip had also allowed her to buy new leather luggage, and each day she added her latest acquisition to the large case or the two smaller ones. Everything looked so new and perfect. She knew that on the last day she would mar the picture by throwing in a few of her old comfy clothes—certainly her warmup suit and sneakers—for relaxed moments.

Otherwise, Sandy was spending the time as she was now, curled up on her couch, preparing for her duties as bodyguard to the Senator. Whether he wanted it or not, his safety on this trip was going to be in the hands of a woman, and that woman was going to be well-prepared.

Snug under the colorful checkerboard wool afghan she had knitted herself, Sandy worked her way through the mound of papers that covered every inch of her glass-topped coffee table. She studied the detailed plans of each deck of the *Voyager Queen*. It was so well equipped and beautifully laid out, it was practically a floating city.

She memorized the location of every cabin and facility. If anyone were to attempt to endanger the Senator in his cabin, Sandy knew all possible approaches, all possible escape routes. She knew all about the key personnel who would staff the vessel. She would need the cooperation of several of them to insure the Senator's safety. In the kitchen, for example, she would assign responsibility for screening food brought to the Senator's table to one of the senior chefs. The stewards on the Senator's deck would have to be briefed and alerted to keep constant watch on his cabin even when he wasn't in it.

Though most of the passengers on the cruise seemed to be retired people, simple and harmless enough, it was Sandy's job to cover all fronts, and she looked over the material Foster Milner had sent her with care. Thorough preparation was her byword.

But this preparation was different. There was inter-
ference caused by an image in her mind, an image that
kept swimming between her and the words on the papers
in front of her. This time there was Senator Rexford...

In the last days before her departure, as she studied
the map of the islands dotting the warm waters of the
South Pacific, the memory of the touch of his lips sent
excited shivers of expectation up and down her spine as
she sat huddled in her chilly, inadequately heated apartment.

All she needed to do was to close her eyes to bring
back the sense of electric intimacy from their few short
moments together—the smell of the leather in the limousine, the dark of the Capitol building closet. Then the
rest would come rushing back—the pressure of his body;
the strength of his arms; his clean, masculine scent.

Sandy forced herself to focus on the dossiers of the
several persons on the Senator's staff who would be
travelling with him. But she had no trouble putting her
mind on his. In fact, she knew the Senator's well-worn
file almost by heart.

> *6'2"*
> *175 lbs.;*
> *black hair;*
> *brown eyes;*
> *scion of distinguished political family;*
> *educated Choate, Harvard, the London School*
> *of Economics;*
> *worked as troubleshooter for family's far-flung*
> *business interests;*
> *U. S. Congressman from California—one term;*
> *U. S. Senator from California—one term;*
> *unmarried;*

His dossier was full of newspaper and magazine clippings that covered his political and personal life of the

past few years. Sandy read every word several times over. She noted that, when he had run for Senator six years ago, Kenneth Rexford had been thirty years old, meeting the age requirements for that office by just a few months. They might be in different leagues in most ways, but simple mathematics told her that, at twenty-eight, she was somewhat in his generation.

The dossier included many clippings of articles and comment on his resignation of his Senate seat last August. There was his own claim that he needed to be free of political duties to carry out a major expansion of his family business, whose interests were worldwide. There was the contention that he had chosen not to run again in order to avoid the notoriety a campaign might bring to light. Through all the comment was the thought that this had been an odd move for a man viewed by most politicians as obvious presidential timber.

His private life was the subject of a wealth of rumor and a great deal of scandal, all unproven, Sandy noted. Time after time the scandal sheets had linked him romantically with starlets and models, and time after time he was forced to protest his innocence. It was a refrain that ran through his entire public life. How could there help but be *some* fire, Sandy wondered, where there was so much smoke? As she pondered the entries in the Senator's file and recalled the sardonic look in his piercing eyes when they had first glimpsed each other in the Rotunda of the Capitol, Sandy grew increasingly nervous at the prospect of her new assignment. Moreover, for the first time in her professional life, she wondered if, after all, she was really prepared for her tasks. And she even felt dubious and apprehensive about her own motivations.

For the first time in a long year, Sandy hadn't thought about her young husband's tragic death for several hours, maybe even days at a time. The resounding crack of Philly's rifle as he tripped over a fallen tree limb in the salty marshes of Delaware, where they had gone for that weekend with several other Secret Service officers and their wives, had not begun her mornings. For a week, she had not gone to sleep hearing that sound reverberating in her head.

Sandy did not know whether to feel relief or guilt. What were her obligations to poor Philly's memory? What were her obligations to herself, to her own future? It had not occurred to her until recently that she actually had one.

If she could barely handle the idea that she had a life to live when Philly did not, what would she do if the time ever came when she and the Senator were suddenly alone on some romantic South Sea island? If he was moved to kiss her in a broom closet, what would "come naturally" to him under swaying palm trees and tropical moonlight?

The Senator was outrageous. He was an insult to Sandy's own decency. Obviously, the tabloids were right about the man. He had no more self-control than a . . . a . . . Or was she wishing that her own upbringing hadn't been so sheltered? Senator Rexford's free-wheeling approach to women was nothing like her own inhibited, monogamous attitude toward men. Philly had been the only one. She hadn't even thought of sleeping with another man, before or since. A shot of anxiety pierced her chest. Maybe she wasn't the person for this job after all.

Sometimes she was tempted to reach for the phone to call Foster and beg to be taken off the assignment. After all, she rehearsed to herself, even his chief aide, that Kenneally fellow, didn't want her along, and thought she'd be bad for the Senator's reputation.

But each time, before she picked up the telephone, something always stopped her. It was too good an opportunity for her, she would admonish herself, without daring to figure out just *which* opportunity she meant.

And so, almost before she knew it, the time came to finish her packing. Alongside the last of her new evening gowns, in and around the two print sundresses with French labels, Sandy packed her karate uniform, her billy club, walkie talkie, gas mask, and the shoulder holster carrying her Police Special.

Everything was ready, organized enough ahead of time to make her departure smooth and easy. She called a cab, left the key to her apartment with a neighbor across the hall, who would water the plants and feed the goldfish, and amidst yet another flurry of snowflakes, not all that common for Washington winters, she instructed the driver to take her to Dulles Airport. Her new assignment, and her new life, were about to begin.

But fate, in the form of the worst blizzard to strike Washington, D. C. in fifteen years, intervened. And instead of winging westward, Sandy found herself spending the night in a cramped seat in the Dulles departure lounge. The hours ticked away, measured by the wind-whipped snowflakes and the howling wind. She knew it was lucky the Agency's West Coast office had taken care of the actual physical checking out of the ship, its passengers and crew, to make certain no obvious bombs or bomb-throwers were aboard. Otherwise, the storm would have been the end of her assignment. As it was, if one more thing went wrong, her job would definitely be in jeopardy.

Finally, the flight was cleared for takeoff during a break in the bad weather. *If* the plane made it to Los Angeles on schedule, and *if* she could find a taxi to the port without delay, she would arrive at the pier from which the *Voyager Queen* would depart with just minutes to spare. If it all went smoothly, Sandy was about to be propelled into the future—whether or not she was ready for it.

4

THE SHIP DIDN'T disappoint Sandy. It loomed up and up and up from its Long Beach berth like the seagoing skyscraper it was.

The taxi from the Los Angeles airport had deposited her at dockside just moments before the beginning of the voyage. Still wearing her down coat and feeling bedraggled after the long, arduous, cross-country flight and surrounded by crowds of tanned, happy people in short-sleeved, colorful clothing, Sandy couldn't have felt more out of place if she had been an Eskimo plunked down in the middle of the Sahara desert. Sandy thought the people on the crowded pier all looked as if they had been sent over from Hollywood Central Casting to play the parts of society swells out for their umpteenth ocean voyage on the royal yacht. Even when she unveiled her new wardrobe, she doubted she could match their panache.

Sandy paused glumly, hefting her bags and looking around her. People with smiling faces shouldered past her. Nearby voices babbled in the cacophony of different languages. Near the gangway she spotted a handsome young man wearing a straw boater, a striped seersucker jacket, and white slacks. He looked like someone straight out of the 1920's, and he was waving madly in her direction. Puzzled, Sandy started tentatively toward him.

"Are you waving at me?" she asked, when she was within a few steps of the young man.

From above, at the head of the gangway, an amplified

voice called out, *"Cut!* Cut, cut, *cut!"* A red-faced bald man in a sweat-stained silk shirt was glaring down at her, a megaphone in his hand.

The young man next to her took off his straw hat and wiped his brow with the back of his hand. He gave her a crooked grin. "You didn't know about this movie, did you?" he asked.

Embarrassed, Sandy shook her head.

"Are you coming aboard for the cruise?"

"Uh-huh," Sandy said, completely puzzled by the turn of events.

"I'll bet you didn't look in your cruise guide," the young man stated accusingly, with a faintly superior air. "You know, the part about how everybody was supposed to be on board an hour early to watch the movie company shoot the big farewell scene?"

"The big farewell scene?" Sandy repeated, unable to recall any cruise guide among her many papers.

"Right," the young man said. "For *Waves of Passion*—that's the name of our film—a real tearjerker, too. We're going to film the whole thing aboard the *Voyager Queen*. The entire company's going to be along on the first half of the cruise. We're one of the big attractions. I mean, *everybody's* watching," he added proudly, crooking his thumb back over his shoulder. "They say that even Senator Rexford's up there."

Horrified, Sandy looked up—and up—and up. Amused faces lined all the deck rails. The crowds around her on the pier seemed to have vanished, she suddenly noticed. She and the man were all alone, except for a strikingly beautiful young woman in a frilly, long white dress, who stood a few feet away, looking exasperated, her hands on her hips.

"Can we get on with this, Miles?" she asked poutingly. "I can't wait to get out of this horrible corset."

"Sure thing, Rose," the young man said. He turned his attention back to Sandy, giving her an appraising look. "I'm Miles," he said. "Miles Moore." He looked clearly crestfallen when it was obvious that his name didn't ring a bell with her.

"I haven't been to the movies much recently," Sandy said apologetically.

Just then, a uniformed steward appeared at her side. "Have you booked passage, madam?" he asked, somewhat disdainfully. When Sandy nodded yes, he asked to see her ticket.

While she was fumbling in her shoulder bag, Miles continued to give her a long, searching look. "Are you in the biz?" he asked at last, running a hand through his blond hair while she handed her ticket over to the steward.

"The biz?" Sandy repeated.

"Yeah, you know, show biz."

"No," Sandy replied carefully, wanting to preserve whatever was left of her low profile.

Beside her, the steward seemed to come to attention. His entire manner toward her seemed to change. "Oh, Senator Rexford's party. I do hope there wasn't any inconvenience." Immediately, he picked up her bags. "This way, please, miss," he added, half-bowing as he started up the gangway.

As Sandy began to follow him up, Miles called after her, "You oughta be in movies, you know. Come talk to me about it. C-Deck, okay? Ask anybody. Miles Moore on C-Deck, where the movie company's staying. Come talk to me about your movie career, okay?"

Sandy turned, waved over her shoulder, and turned up the corners of her mouth in a faint smile. "Sure," she said without much conviction. "Bye."

The obsequious steward led her past the angry, bullet-headed man with the megaphone at the head of the gangway. Sandy noticed that he was peering at her through something in his hand that looked like a camera lens and was mumbling to himself in a faintly Germanic accent.

"Interesting," he said as she passed. *"Sehr* interesting. I vant that girl's name."

"A-Deck is our Sun Deck," the steward explained, while he and Sandy rode up one of the ship's elevators. "Right below the bridge and it has the choicest rooms. The Senator's party has several connecting suites, all with a large central sitting room, wardrobe rooms and, of course, terraces with excellent sea views."

"Of course," Sandy repeated distractedly, not really listening to the steward's enthusiastic description. She felt mortified. Everyone had seen the embarrassing way she'd come aboard the ship, traipsing obliviously through the movie scene like that. No doubt even Senator Rexford had been watching from the upper deck, probably with that same amused, sardonic look that had been haunting her dreams for the last three weeks.

"This way, please," the steward said, when the elevator doors opened. He led her down a long, plush-carpeted hallway. At the far end, a line of uniformed stewards, each carrying a suitcase or wheeling a dolly with a large trunk on it, was waiting at a doorway. "Your suites are all the way forward, miss. They have an un-impeded view. The Senator has the presidential suite, and you'll be in the Regency, right next to Mrs. Winston."

"Mrs. Winston?"

Sandy immediately recognized the name of Senator Rexford's sister, Amelia Rexford Winston. She had read the dossier just the other day. The woman had been married to Marshall Winston, the shipping mogul, who had recently died of a heart attack. Somehow the thought of practically sharing quarters with the elegant woman seemed somewhat overwhelming.

"Yes, miss, these are some of her things," the steward said happily, indicating all the chests, suitcases, and boxes that the other men were carrying into the stateroom. "It's been years since the line has seen luxury like this on the

Pacific run," he added, escorting her past the line of uniformed men and putting her two plain bags just inside.

Sandy stepped hesitantly into the large, richly furnished, wood-panelled sitting room. There, an elegantly dressed woman coiffed in a perfect pageboy of prematurely gray hair, was supervising as the trunks were brought inside. As soon as she saw Sandy standing in the doorway, she turned from directing the stewards and strode briskly toward her, her long, perfectly manicured hand extended in greeting. The light caught the smooth white of the long, single strand of pearls around her neck.

"My dear, how pleased I am to see you," she said in a voice as richly cultured as the simple black dress she wore was tailored and elegant. "May I call you Sandy?"

"Of—of course," Sandy replied graciously, but in an obviously puzzled tone of voice. It was taking a moment for all that she had read in the dossiers to piece itself together. How did Mrs. Winston know her name?

"Oh, how rude of me!" the elegant woman said immediately. "Obviously, you're Sandy O'Hara—my brother mentioned that you are the one who is assigned to him for this . . . mission and that we'd be sharing this suite. I'm Amelia Winston," she smiled and leaned forward confidentially, a big smile on her long, aristocratic face, which suddenly looked familiar to Sandy. "Kenny's my *younger* brother," she said with a wink, "but don't tell anybody. It isn't good for either of our images. You know how it is when you're on a sea cruise to get over a tragic love affair," she added mysteriously.

Sandy smiled, she hoped with understanding, though she wasn't quite sure whether or not Amelia Winston was referring to her own recent widowhood. She chose to look businesslike and said, "I should probably report to the Senator right away, Mrs. Winston. Do you know where I can find him?"

Amelia pointed to a closed door. "He's in the connecting cabin, in the presidential suite, having a confer-

ence with his aides—Kenneally and Harvey, that young
fellow I don't know very well. They're talking politics
and planning strategy and that sort of thing. Why don't
you just let him continue with his meeting..."

"But why?" Sandy asked, immediately afraid she had
sounded almost petulant in her eagerness to see the man
who had been in her thoughts almost constantly since
the day she had spoken with him.

"Well, I know they have important matters to settle
and will want to be closeted in there for hours. There's
plenty of time to 'report in' over dinner tonight at the
Captain's table."

"The Captain's table?" Sandy asked. Now she probably sounded totally ignorant.

"Yes, dear. There was an invitation in Ken's cabin
when we boarded, inviting him and his party to spend
the first evening out at the Captain's table. We have
accepted of course. I do so love shipboard evenings,"
Amelia continued obliviously. "Formal clothes, everything so romantic and elegant." She paused, her eyes
focusing on Sandy's three leather bags where the porter
had placed them just inside the door. "I'm sure you came
equipped with a formal wardrobe?"

"Yes, I'm prepared, Mrs. Winston, for just about
anything."

"I'm sure you are, dear. I was so impressed to learn
that Ken's personal bodyguard would be a woman...even
if he...well, you know. Men underestimate the abilities
of women, don't they, even in this day and age when
women are doing well in all sorts of professions. Don't
let it worry you though. He'll come around."

A flash of anger coursed through Sandy as she rec-
ollected her last encounter with Senator Rexford. "If
you would like to be replaced...reconsider this assignment..." he'd said. One way or another, she would show
him that she was a force to be reckoned with.

To Amelia Winston she said, "There aren't many

women in the protective services yet. It's probably hard to get used to the idea."

Mrs. Winston's festive mood suddenly seemed gone. The corners of her mouth began to quiver slightly. "My Marshall..." she began. "He was always supportive of my efforts. Though I've never been employed, I've always had my hand in any number of charities, you know. Marshall always said..."

But Sandy was not to know what Marshall always said. Amelia Winston covered her face with her long, delicate fingers and slumped into a chair. She sobbed quietly, her shoulders shaking gently, her grief strumming the string of Sandy's own and bringing a large lump to her throat. She went to the older woman and put a hand on her shoulder.

"It's hard to lose someone you love. I've just been widowed for a year myself, Mrs. Winston," she said softly.

The older woman looked up at her. "Yes, Ken told me, dear," she said. The Senator had obviously been reading Sandy's dossier too.

Amelia Winston took a lace handkerchief from the alligator purse by her side and wiped her eyes in two swift strokes. "Well," she said, "we'll have a great deal in common, my dear. We can be of comfort to each other."

There was a needy, almost imploring tone in her voice that seemed at odds with her elegant bearing. "I'd appreciate that, Mrs. Winston." Sandy smiled.

"Do call me Amelia, dear. I'm sure we will become great friends."

5

DINNER THAT FIRST night at sea was a splendid black-tie affair. On a sea voyage of such length, by tradition, all the first-class passengers would eventually take a turn at the Captain's table in the Grand Ballroom. But to dine with Captain McCabe on the first night was a special honor.

Amelia wore a dazzling gown of glittering gold lamé. Sandy had chosen a two-piece evening dress in dramatic black silk. The dress had a bias-cut neckline that left one shoulder bare, and around her waist was a wide belt of gleaming beaten gold. "You look simply beautiful, dear," Amelia had told her admiringly in the shared sitting room between their suites. "Black brings out the healthy glow of your skin and highlights that golden hair of yours, which, of course, I'd kill to have myself."

Looking at herself in the mirror, Sandy just smiled. She had to admit that the dress was the perfect choice, and her gruelling shopping trips all over Washington in the weeks before she'd left began to seem worthwhile.

After only a few hours with Amelia, Sandy was already enjoying her company and coming to think of the older woman as a friend. Amelia had fine judgment and her every move seemed polished and gracious. Somehow, without seeming to make any effort at all, she had contrived to have Sandy and herself arrive in the ballroom just the precisely correct number of minutes late. Everyone else was seated at the Captain's big round table in the center of the dining room. Only their two chairs were empty. White-haired Captain McCabe was there, looking every inch the commander in his white dress uniform with gold buttons and black epaulets. An obviously *nouveau riche* tourist couple was there—she was overweight and wearing a most unflattering pink-chiffon gown. He was boisterous and had on a dark, filigreed Western suit and a spaghetti string tie. Crusty Fitzpatrick Kenneally, looking utterly uncomfortable in formal dress, was present, along with one of the assistant political aides—Harvey Cattler—an owlish, sallow young man wearing wire-rimmed glasses, who, Amelia whispered as they approached the table, was passionate about "facts, figures and politics—and *nothing else*."

And there was the Senator, dark and distinguished. He was the obvious focus of attention at the table. In fact, heads were turning in his direction from all over the dining room. His bearing was erect, his gestures were refined yet natural, and he looked completely at ease in his perfectly tailored tuxedo.

Sandy felt the blood rush to her face as his eyes met hers. She detected the slightest of nods in her direction, and then saw him raise his hand gently to Amelia as they approached, all the while continuing his conversation. The men at the table rose as one as she and Amelia drew closer, the Senator rising to his full height.

"Ladies." Captain McCabe gave a courtly bow and offered the red-leather armchair next to him. Before Sandy could make a move, Amelia had taken the chair herself. That left only one place vacant, the chair next to Senator Rexford, who now seemed to be sending a suggestive, slanted smile at her from the other side of the elegantly set table. Without letting her eyes meet his again, Sandy moved beside the proffered chair beside him. "I'm Sandy O'Hara," she said after Amelia had introduced herself to everyone.

"Hello again," the Senator said in a husky whisper, as they all resumed their seats.

"I didn't know if you'd been able to get out from under Washington's snowdrifts. I've been out here a few days myself."

"Yes," Sandy said, daring to look up at him briefly. "I've been caught in quite a few snowstorms this winter."

She was surprised at herself, breaking her vow already, alluding almost flirtatiously to their last meeting. She groaned silently to herself. She certainly was getting off to a bad start.

"But you escaped from all of them none the worse for wear?" The Senator grinned down at her. Lowering his voice to a whisper, he added, "And here you are, ready for duty. Are you all prepared to keep me well-protected?"

There was a definite sneer in his tone, and Sandy was reminded that she was up against more than one kind of challenge with this man. Keeping him at bay physically was one. The other was more crucial. She had to convince him to take her seriously as a professional.

Sandy barely heard Captain McCabe's introductions, or noticed when the stewards set steaming bowls of creamy bisque on the table and poured a sparkling Sauvignon Blanc into the crystal stemware. She was marshalling her strength to deal with the man who sat next to her.

She was determined not to notice his tanned hand resting lightly on the edge of the table, just a fraction of an inch away from her own. She ignored the way the cuff of his trousers brushed against her ankle when he shifted imperceptibly in his seat. She refused to take in the fact that once or twice his upper arm touched her bare shoulder as he moved. She was so intent on not inhaling the bracing scent of his after-shave lotion that she barely breathed at all.

The loud man in the western suit was looking in Sandy and the Senator's direction from where he sat at the end of the table. He was talking expansively about himself— going on about his business and his hobby of photography—but Sandy was listening only to the booming beat of her heart.

"Hartmann's," he was saying. "Surely even ya'll in Washington have heard of us. The biggest little department store in the great state of Texas!" He patted his wife's plump hand. "The little woman's the buyer, and I run the whole shebang. We're the ones first came up with a ritzy, chic-y Christmas catalogue. 'Course, nowadays, everybody's copyin' it, but we were first. And this year, this very cruise was our top-of-the-line item. Guess nobody could afford it—a bit pricey at a hundred grand for two, huh? So me and the little lady decided the best way to get our investment back was to hop on and take the cruise ourselves! Great idea, huh?"

"Yeah, great," Fitzpatrick Kenneally growled, pulling uncomfortably on the tight collar of his ruffled white shirt. "Say you're goin' to be on board for the whole cruise, is that so?" he added acerbically in his Irish brogue.

Amelia interjected smoothly, "Why, I've shopped from your catalogue a number of times, Mr. Hartmann."

But the obstreperous Texan ignored both the compliment and Kenneally's dig. His narrow eyes focused on Sandy's face. "Say, Miss O'Hara, haven't I seen you someplace before?" he drawled, squinting closely at her. "Yer the purrtiest little thing, ain't ya? You must be in the movies or somethin'. Hey, that's it, I saw you with that movie-show company this afternoon. Hey, you're an actress, right, little lady?"

Sandy felt out of touch with the whole proceedings. Somehow someone had whisked away her unfinished bisque and now a plate with stuffed trout and spears of fresh asparagus covered with rich Hollandaise sauce was in front of her. Everyone else seemed to have almost finished eating, and for some reason they were all looking at her.

"Mr. Hartmann says he thinks you're an actress,"

Amelia prompted smoothly from across the table. "Isn't that amusing?"

"No, no, Mr. Hartmann," Sandy blurted out. "I'm not. At least, not yet." It suddenly occurred to her that it might not be a bad idea to let people think the movie being filmed was her major interest aboard the ship.

"A film career would be very exciting, I'm sure," she went on. "And I seem to be mistaken for an actress quite often. I used to act in plays in school, but at the moment, that is not my career."

"Why then, whatever *do* you do, young lady?" Mr. Hartmann queried persistently. "You gotta be *real special* to be here, y'know."

"Well," Sandy began hesitantly, not at all certain how much she should reveal about her assignment. What would *he* want her to say?

Again Amelia stepped in to assist her. "Why, Sandy's with my brother and me."

"Your brother?" Hartmann repeated. "Oh, *the Senator*," he said, a suggestive, insinuating look crossing his face. "I see. I *see*..."

Sandy felt Ken Rexford stiffen next to her. "No, Mr. Hartmann, I really don't think you do. Your tone suggests you might be thinking of some of that unpleasant publicity I've been receiving in the tabloids lately. Surely you don't believe everything you read in the press?"

"I wouldn't vote for you, if that's what you mean," Hartmann countered, ignoring his wife's warning hand on his arm.

The Senator chuckled urbanely. "I can't say I'm too surprised. After all, I've always numbered among my opponents such narrow-mi—"

"His bodyguard," Kenneally cut in without hesitation. "Ms. O'Hara is the Senator's bodyguard."

"Huh?" The Texas entrepreneur turned to the haggard-faced political aide with amazement in his voice. "His *bodyguard?*" he repeated incredulously.

"Yes," Kenneally said levelly with a sigh. "Ms. O'Hara is a highly trained, competent professional, very respected by her peers."

Hartmann guffawed openly. He pointed a stubby finger directly at Sandy's face. "This willowy young thing is a *bodyguard?* I wonder what kind of guarding of the Senator's body she'll be up to!"

The pudgy Texan leaned back, his hands on the edge of the table, the front legs of his chair tipped off the floor, to give him room for a long, loud belly laugh.

Sandy knew this was not the time or the place. The Texan's assault on the Senator was only mildly abusive, but his innuendoes as to her purpose on this trip infuriated her.

Though there were several people between her and where Mr. Hartmann sat at the end of the table, Sandy's trained eye told her that one sharp pull of the tablecloth, which was all that was between the mirth-filled Texan and the table he held for balance, would land him squarely on his backside on the floor.

Calculating her move in a flash, designing its direction so that crystal glasses would not fall into each other, Sandy reached with both hands into the center of the table. Her split-second yank pulled the cloth out from under his grasp with such force that it was apparent to hardly anyone at the table what had happened. All they could see was that Mr. Hartmann had gone over backwards in a resounding crash of splintering wood. Only one water glass had gone over in the process, and Sandy reached hastily to right it, before any more than a damp spot was left.

All eyes were focused at the end of the table. Mrs. Hartmann rose to her feet, rushing to help her fallen husband, who seemed as unable to move as an overturned turtle. The only eyes on Sandy were the Senator's, and they sparkled with amusement. His hand went up to cover the grin that was bursting across his face.

Captain McCabe rose to help Mrs. Hartmann lift her husband to his feet and waved to a waiter, who cleared away the debris of the broken chair.

Sandy sipped demurely at her wine, as though nothing had happened.

"I'm glad that you are all right, Mr. Hartmann," Amelia was saying politely, as the hefty man straightened his dinner jacket and tie and his wife brushed him off in back.

"Well," he drawled, "I guess they just don't make those ballroom chairs the way they used to." Apparently he had forgotten the subject of his earlier amusement.

Just then, the discordant sounds of musical instruments tuning up behind them drew the attention of all the diners away from the table.

"Our first dance at sea," Captain McCabe said, as the ship's orchestra struck up a spirited waltz. He stood and offered his hand to Amelia. "Mrs. Winston, would you do me the honor?"

"Of course," Amelia said, looking pleased and radiant, as she stood to take the Captain's hand. Soon they were twirling around the polished floor of the band area on the other side of the large ballroom.

Mercifully, the Hartmanns, too, headed for a turn around the dance floor.

Kenneally, staring after them, shook his head in disbelief and sighed. "I need a drink," he growled to the owlish assistant aide. "C'mon, Harvey, let's go to the ship's saloon." Soon they, too, had left.

For a moment Sandy and the Senator sat side by side in silence.

"Well, Ms. O'Hara," he said, "you seem to have come to my defense again."

"I've learned a few tricks in my years in this business, Senator." She smiled at him over the edge of her wine glass.

"Is that how lady bodyguards deal with aggressors

larger and stronger than they are? With a flick of the wrist?"

"Whenever possible," she answered. Sandy felt herself beaming up at him with a mixture of pride in herself and awe at him. She adjusted her expression. She definitely had the upper hand at this moment, and she might as well hang on to it for as long as possible.

"Well, let's hope there is always a tablecloth between me and my assailants in the future. Then I'll never have a thing to worry about."

Sandy drew herself up in her chair. "Senator Rexford, I think you will find I am up to this job, even if I do have to grapple with someone three times my size. Size doesn't necessarily reveal strength, you know. Most of it is mental, and I have a well-trained mind. I advise you to get used to the idea that you have a female bodyguard and relax."

"All I can do is promise to try. By the way, *Ms*. O'Hara, most people who work closely with me do not call me *Senator* Rexford. I'm Ken, if that's okay with you?"

"All right, and you might as well call me Sandy..."

"Good. I was hoping you'd say that," he replied, sounding suddenly friendly. This man ran as hot and cold as spring weather. "Now, just a couple more points. One, Fitzpatrick Kenneally is Fitz. You'll only confuse him if you call him *Mister* Kenneally. Is that understood?"

Sandy nodded tightly.

"He is more opposed to having you along on this trip than I am, so that may be as friendly as you'll ever get with him, but it might help."

"Senator... I mean, Ken, I well understand that no one is exactly cheering for me around here. But you and your aide are going to make my job a lot harder if you continue to point it out to me. And now, if you'll excuse me..." Sandy pushed her chair back from the table.

"Not so fast, Sandy." He gave her an engagingly

boyish grin, probably the one he had perfected to win over reluctant voters.

"If there isn't anything in the bodyguards' code of conduct that prohibits it," he said in the sonorous voice of a politician, "I would like to ask you to dance."

Sandy smiled in spite of herself. She didn't really feel like leaving the party, and he was her client. "The situation hasn't come up often in the past," she said slowly, "so I don't suppose there's anything to stop us."

But there *was* something to stop her. The very thought of being in the arms of this exasperatingly inconsistent man, who made fun of her one minute and wanted to kiss her the next.

But it was too late. He was standing and helping Sandy from the chair, adding, "If it gets very crowded on that dance floor after all, I might need official protection."

Now he was laughing at her again. There was only one safe way to deal with Ken Rexford, Sandy reminded herself—set herself on "professional," and never look to one side or the other. That was what she was going to do.

Soon they were gliding across the dance floor together, his arms around her, holding her chest to his, her head tucked under his chin. Despite all her resolve to see herself only as his bodyguard, she had to admit that she felt suddenly warm and secure and safe in his arms.

They danced wordlessly together, while all around them swirled other couples coming onto the little dance floor to follow the lead of the Captain's table. Close together, moving gracefully as one in time to the spirited music, Sandy had the oddest feeling. Their bodies spoke volumes; it was as if they'd been talking together for years.

She was becoming more and more aware of the pressure of his hand on her back, of the nearness of his handsome face, and of how his body kept inching ever closer to hers as they danced. She knew that if she didn't strike up some sort of conversation soon, her whole body would betray her with its unspoken desires.

It had been so long since Philly...since they had made love. His face came before her now as she remembered their high school prom, so many years ago. They were dancing when he had first said it out loud, the thought that had been between them all through high school. "Someday, Sandy, I want you to be my wife."

She stiffened and pulled back from Ken's broad chest. The orchestra swung into a second melody, and Sandy searched her brain wildly for something to say, words to put between them. "About the way we met—in the Capitol—and then, in your limousine, Ken, I want you to know that *I* am not in the habit of—"

"As I told you," Ken interrupted her, "neither am I, Sandy." He held her tightly and danced in silence.

We all know about that, she thought to herself, and let the subject drop.

Once more they danced. In spite of the thoughts in Sandy's head, their bodies seemed to be carrying on in eloquent conversation as they moved perfectly together through the steps of the waltz.

They whirled past Amelia and the Captain, who were still dancing, and once again the Senator whispered, speaking quickly as if unburdening himself of a heavy secret. "Amelia's husband died a year ago—just like yours. That's another reason for this trip—to bring her back into the world of pleasure and sunlight. I asked that her stateroom adjoin yours hoping you would become friends."

Sandy was about to reply, but just then the orchestra conductor turned to the microphone at the front of the little stage and called out, "Everybody! Change partners!" Immediately the orchestra began to play a tango. To much laughter and applause from everyone in the ballroom, the dancers all turned away from their partners and began dancing with whoever was close by.

Sandy found herself facing Captain McCabe. "Ms. O'Hara," he said, gallantly offering his arms.

"My pleasure, Captain," she said, stepping forward.

The Captain's weathered face was creased in momentary thought as they took their turn around the floor. "Ms. O'Hara," he began courteously, "this ship represents something new for the Petropolis Line, and for the entire shipping industry. It's a return to the kind of luxury ocean travel that hasn't been seen, at its best, since before the War. That's why I want to apologize to you for the behavior of Mr. Hartmann at table tonight, and its crashing denouement, as it were.

"No matter how valuable his advertising services are to the company, such rudeness is inexcusable. I'm well aware of your superior qualifications for your duties on this voyage, and as Captain I appreciate the Senator's efforts not to alarm the other passengers with obvious security precautions."

Sandy was impressed by Captain McCabe's considerateness. That he would make the effort to reassure her said something about his character that Sandy liked. She was about to thank him and tell him the truth about Mr. Hartmann's fall, when the orchestra leader again called out, "Change partners! Everybody!"

Sandy turned, pleased to see out of the corner of her eye that Ken was nearby and was about to come toward her. But another couple was nearby, too—Miles and his co-star, the impatient, dark-haired beauty, Rose.

Rose stepped quickly directly in front of Ken, and just as quickly, Miles stepped over to Sandy and swept her out onto the dance floor as the orchestra began an uptempo Latin rhythm.

Sandy had to admit to herself that fair-haired, athletic-looking Miles Moore wore a tuxedo well, almost as well as Ken Rexford. There was a youthfulness and simplicity about Miles that reminded her a little of Philly. He, too, had remained a boy all his life. It was not necessarily a bad quality in either a peace officer or a movie star, she decided. At any rate, the resemblance to Philly made her feel more at ease with Miles.

"Hi, Miles," she said with a friendly smile as they began to dance together. "I didn't think I'd see you again so soon."

Without preamble, Miles responded in a stage whisper, "Everyone's talking!"

"Really? About what, Miles?" Sandy asked, amused by his immediate theatrics.

"They want to know who that beautiful creature with Senator Rexford is. I told Babs Teller I knew you personally. Even my director is intrigued."

"Do you mean me?" Sandy asked incredulously. "And who's Babs Teller?"

Miles clicked his tongue in disbelief. "Don't you watch TV either?"

"Well, now that you mention it, recently I've been kind of too busy for much—"

"*Barbara* Teller, the television gossip columnist, that name doesn't ring a bell with you? Honestly, some people have no idea how lucky they are, just no idea at all."

"Miles, what *are* you talking about?"

"Babs Teller, that's what I'm talking about. She's on this cruise until Australia—to interview the movie company, to tape some bits for her show. You know, that sort of thing. She was at our table tonight, and all she could talk about is the Senator. All she was interested in was *you*. The Mystery Woman, she kept calling you. I could practically see the wheels spinning in her head."

Sandy laughed nervously. It was all too ridiculous, but it was disturbing nonetheless to be the object of a gossip columnist's curiosity when she was supposed to be keeping a low profile.

"Be serious," Miles whispered loudly. "This could be very good for your career."

"*Career?*" Sandy repeated. "What career are you talking about? I have a perfectly good career already."

"Why, in show business, of course," Miles said,
sounding a little affronted. "I told Babs I'd promised to
help you get your start. She was *very* impressed. Now,
why don't you just give her an interview, then I'm sure
our director . . ."

Sandy was horrified. If it had crossed her mind that
letting people think she was interested in a movie career
was a good decoy, the need for that was over. Kenneally
had announced loud and clear at the table that she was
the Senator's bodyguard. "Miles! Absolutely not! I never
told you any such—"

"Shhh! Look!" As they swung around the dance floor,
he nodded surreptitiously in the direction of a tiny, sharp-
eyed woman standing in a corner talking animatedly to
none other than the loud and hostile Mr. Hartmann.
"That's her," Miles whispered admiringly. "Look at her
go. You can tell when that lady's dishing the dirt from
a mile away."

Sandy's heart seemed to fall all the way into the pit
of her stomach. What had she gotten herself into! What
scandals would Hartmann insinuate, and what would it
do to Ken and to Amelia?

"Miles, I'd like to go up to my room now," Sandy
said abruptly, too upset to be aware of the effect her
words had on the youthful movie actor. "I—I don't think
I feel very well."

Miles gave her a crooked grin. "Sure thing, babes,
I'll take you up. I'd like to have a look at how the better
half lives up on A-Deck anyway," he said, placing her
hand in the crook of his elbow and escorting her off the
dance floor with a self-assured swagger.

Sandy was too disconcerted to protest, and noticed
only fleetingly that on the other side of the dance floor
Ken, now dancing with his sister, followed her sudden
departure with a look of concern. Sandy was more aware
of the piercing eyes of the gossip columnist watching her

every move as she and Miles made their exit. But all she heard was what Miles had told her when they had first started their dance. *Everyone's talking*, he had whispered. *Everyone's talking* . . .

6

"WOW-EE, LOOK AT that view! It's like Cinerama up here, or 3-D. This is the high life, isn't it? Down on C-Deck the actors just get little cubicles, cells practically. But then again, we're really just the hired help."

As soon as Sandy had taken out her stateroom key, Miles had made a great show of gallantry by taking it out of her hand and opening the door. Now he handed it back to her with a little flourish and a small, mocking bow. "Mind if I come in?" he said over his shoulder as he stepped inside. "Just look at that terrace," he added, crossing the dimly lit sitting room to gaze out the double glass doors. "Just look at that," he repeated. "Stars! Moonlight! The ocean liner's bow cutting through the sea! What a scene!"

When the brazen, young movie actor turned around, he was already loosening his bow tie and unfastening the top stud of his dress shirt. The same crooked little smile Sandy had noticed before flashed across his chiseled leading-man features. In the half-darkness of the sitting room, he looked at her through hooded eyes, seeming to gaze at her without really seeing her at all. "How about a drink, Sandy?" he suggested in a husky whisper. He took a couple of steps back toward where she stood perplexed in the middle of the room.

"Some other time, okay, Miles? It's been an extremely long and trying day, and I'm terribly tired," Sandy said. "And I've got a lot of thinking to do," she added as if to herself.

Miles wagged a finger disapprovingly in front of her face. "You should *never* put off talking about your career." He stepped closer. "Besides, is this any way to treat the man who's going to make you a star?"

"But, Miles, I don't want to—"

"Nonsense!" the mercurial actor snapped, an angry scowl crossing his face. *"Everybody* wants to be a star. Even to think otherwise is—is...practically un-American. Now, c'mon, a pretty, intelligent girl like you *must* be on this ritzy cruise to get discovered. So, let's not kid ourselves. It's just a question of discovered by *whom* and for *what*. I mean, you're not going to be silly enough to hold out for one of these old fuddy-duddy millionaires or that stuffed-shirt senator you were making eyes at before."

"Miles!" Sandy interjected irately, but the actor ignored her protest. He stepped forward again, reaching out for her, and Sandy immediately backed away.

"You're a real looker, babes," he murmured ominously, "but it takes more than that—"

"Miles..."

"Now you just stop playing hard-to-get—you've already played *that* scene to the hilt—and let old Uncle Miles advise you on the ways of Hollywood." Again he stepped forward, and again she backed away.

"Miles, cut it out this instant and come to your senses," she ordered, but it was to no avail. She stepped back as he continued to stalk her openly across the darkened room.

The actor almost seemed to be in a trance. His eyes didn't leave her face once as he came toward her. "A pretty lady like you won't have a bit of trouble getting on in Tinseltown," he whispered reassuringly. "Not with old Uncle Miles to guide you. You'll meet the right people, get the right agent. Why, just think of all the publicity you can get from one Babs Teller interview alone."

Sandy was about to protest again, to say that publicity was the last thing she wanted, and if that didn't work, this young man was going to find out the hard way that she was a trained martial artist, with lethal hands. But the tall actor was looming over her, the room was dark and unfamiliar, and she was continuing to step away.

The wooden arm of the leather couch seemed to come out of nowhere, like a board whacking her across the back of her knees. Her legs flew out from under her as her own momentum knocked her backwards.

"Aah!" With a little cry of surprise, she came down flat on her back on the overstuffed leather couch. Her long legs flew up into the air. The hem of her long black dress bunched up in disarray around her knees. Its thin, black velvet strap slipped off her rounded shoulder. In an instant Miles was on top of her.

The full weight of his body crushed her, knocking the breath from her lungs. His mouth pressed cruelly down against hers. His huge hand pushed the hem of her dress even higher and probed roughly toward the secret places of her body. She twisted and wriggled and, without dislodging Miles a single millimeter, managed to pull them both up to a half-sitting position, sprawling in the center of the couch.

Succumbing to Miles's crude advances was out of the question. His hot touch repelled her. She continued to squirm under him, caught in his passionate grasp, while she hunted for an opening, so she could make a move to free herself without seriously injuring him. It seemed an eternity before she was able to free one arm and bring it around behind his neck.

He seemed to think that she was finally responding to him, and his frenzy increased. With one hand she grasped a shock of his blond hair.

This should do it, she thought grimly. If I have to, I'll pull it out by the dark roots.

She tugged, increasing the pressure gradually. Out of

the side of her pinioned mouth she whispered, "Let go, unless you're ready to become prematurely bald."

Just then a shadow fell across her and Miles—a shadow from the open doorway...

Ken looked stricken. Miles sat bolt upright, an ugly grin on his professionally handsome features. "Why hel-lo, Senator. Didn't expect to find *you* in this little scene," he said awkwardly.

Ken was shaking his head from side to side, as if he didn't believe what he was seeing and could somehow erase the vision before his eyes. "I—I—saw you leave and thought perhaps..."

He held a hand, palm out, in front of him as he backed away. "The door was open. I should've knocked. I—I didn't mean to intrude."

"Wait!" Sandy cried out, jumping up from the couch. "Let me explain!" But it was too late. Ken was gone.

Behind her, Miles reached up and grasped her by the wrist. "Never mind about him," he began, tugging on her arm.

Instinctively, Sandy spun in the direction of his pulling pressure. With her free hand she slapped the presumptuous actor across the face as hard as she could.

"Get out!" she hissed in a voice seething with cold fury. "Or you'll get what you really deserve!" She held her open hand up again, ready to strike.

There was no mistaking her meaning, just as there was no question about whose will would be worked now. Still, Miles tried once more.

"C'mon, babes, you know you want it. You better stay on my good side, honey—"

"And you better get out. *Now.*"

"But..."

"Not one more word, or I'll throw you out! I'm not kidding either."

Miles grimaced and rubbed his sore jaw. He looked as if he might say something else, then just shrugged, stood up, and walked awkwardly from the stateroom.

When he was out of sight and she had closed and locked the door to her cabin, Sandy finally sat down in a corner of the couch and began to cry.

After her mother had died, when she was just a little girl growing up alone in a household full of strong, teasing men, Sandy O'Hara would go up to her small bedroom and cry herself to sleep in secret. That was the time when she first learned there were some things you couldn't tell most people, but especially not to men.

She thought she had outgrown the habit. But the death of the boy she had grown up with—who was like another one of her many older brothers—and married at a young age, had brought back these bouts and sent her to sleep in tears many times in the past year. And now it seemed even the distraught, disappointed look on Ken Rexford's patrician face as he stood aghast in the stateroom doorway could move her to tears.

What conclusions had Ken jumped to, finding her tangled in Miles's embrace, her dress crumpled and half off her body? It was probably not evident to him in the few seconds he had observed them that she, in fact, was struggling to get free of Miles's repulsive embrace. She might as well assume that Ken had thought the worst, though how he could possibly suspect that she had any interest in the pushy actor was beyond her comprehension. Unless, of course, he really thought she had designs on a career as an actress.

After all, when Ken had first seen her in the Rotunda, the man in the tourist group had mistaken her for a movie actress. Mr. Hartmann thought she might be in films, and she had let him think she might have some dream of that sort. If that is what Ken thought, she supposed these incidents had all contributed to the impression.

Sandy tried to recall the exact expression on Ken's face as she looked up from her struggle with Miles. He was obviously shocked, let down, and angry. Betrayed?

Did he look like a man who felt he had been betrayed? That was nonsense, given his own track record with women. He had known Sandy very briefly and certainly wouldn't expect the loyalty of a lover from her.

Sandy sighed deeply. She was very tired, and the situation was more than she could puzzle out. One thing was clear. If Ken had had no confidence in her as his bodyguard before the skirmish with Miles, he definitely wouldn't have any now. He would think of her as some witless, silly woman, interested in the passing attentions of a movie actor, or after a movie career and willing to succumb to any useful man who came her way.

She wasn't sure she could repair the damage. She wasn't sure she could ever gain his respect professionally, given the course things had taken. But then, the whole assignment had been under a cloud from the very beginning, she felt—just as she had been under Ken's spell right from the moment they had first kissed. In her tired, unguarded moments, Sandy had to admit this, at least to herself, however hopeless any feelings she had for him might be.

Was there any way, she wondered, slipping into the short, pink-satin chemise she slept in, that things would seem better in the morning? It was unlikely, she knew, unless somehow Ken Rexford woke up under the illusion that the last scene of the evening had only been part of his dreams.

The sound of the water glass on the night stand next to Sandy's bed crashing to the floor and shattering into a thousand shards startled her out of a dreamless sleep. She slipped a blue cotton robe over her bare shoulders and carefully padded barefoot across the room. Everything seemed most unsteady, she noticed, making her way to the sitting room and then over to the glass doors leading out to the little terrace. What she saw when she gazed out over the bow confirmed her worst suspicions.

The bow of the *Voyager Queen* was plowing through huge, white-tipped waves! Rain lashed the churning gray seas. Wind-whipped storm clouds scudded across the horizon. The ship, Sandy realized, had encountered a sudden strong gale.

A swift gust blew open the terrace door and, before she could get it closed again, Sandy was drenched to the skin. After managing to close and latch the door, she turned, holding her hands behind her back and leaning against the shut doors. While she was catching her breath, Amelia's bedroom door opened and two men came into the room. Ken was first, his black hair tousled and an orange terrycloth robe thrown over his gray silk pajama bottoms. Sandy could tell from the black leather bag he was carrying that the little, gray-haired man behind him was the ship's doctor.

"What's wrong?" she asked immediately, heedless of the fact that her flimsy pink nightie was soaked right through and that her robe was open, exposing her long legs and bare feet. "Is something the matter with Amelia?"

Ken stiffened when he saw her and said nothing. The doctor squinted near-sightedly at her from across the room. "Oh, she'll be fit as a fiddle again," he replied, "soon as all this rolling back and forth stops and we get some calm seas again. A little seasickness never did anybody permanent damage. Just makes you feel miserable as hell. But don't worry, miss," he added as he went out the door, "I gave her some strong sedatives and instructions to take more until we get through this patch of rough weather. Best thing for her would be to sleep right through this storm. Bye now."

"Thank you, Doctor Peters," Ken said as the ship's physician left. "Amelia always did have a fluttery, nervous stomach, even on car trips." Now Ken spoke to Sandy in a subdued voice without looking at her, his dark eyes fixed on a point well to one side of her. "I should've remembered what a bad traveller she can be. I guess I was thinking of other things."

Sandy wiped a damp strand of flaxen hair away from her face. "About last night," she began. "About what you saw. I want to explain." She took a tentative step forward.

"No, no, that's quite all right," Ken responded instantly. "You owe me nothing, least of all an explanation. I should have realized myself. You're a most attractive young woman. It's been a year, I believe, since your husband died. I'm told that young man is an actor, and naturally that would make him very attractive to the opposite sex. So what could be more natural—"

"Ken!" Sandy interjected in a pained voice. "It wasn't that way at all. Please..." She took another step toward him.

He laughed, a bitter, hollow sound. "Really, it's all too absurd," he said. "It's *you* who are supposed to be guarding *me*. But *I* go running after *you* like some concerned schoolboy and come crashing right into your little tryst. I must have looked like a complete idiot standing there and gawking at the two of you. I suppose *I* should apologize."

"Please, Ken, don't," Sandy pleaded, stepping forward again. How could he think she would respond so readily to Miles's advances? "It's all just a mistake. Miles has some plan to help me get started on a career in the movies, but I ..."

The ship's sudden, shuddery lurch caught Sandy by surprise. The bow dipped abruptly, and just as abruptly rose again, like some wildly bucking leviathan determined to throw its small human riders. Caught off balance, Sandy was thrown forward, right into Ken Rexford's outstretched arms.

She smashed up against his chest, her surprised face just inches from his own. His strong arms went around her waist, holding her for support. Then his eyes met hers.

He pulled her closer. His terry bathrobe fell open, and her taut breasts pushed against his bare chest.

She was excruciatingly aware that her wet, flimsy chemise was the only thing keeping her skin from touching his and that his open robe and baggy pajama bottoms left him as nearly naked as she. She could sense his rising passion.

"Oh, Ken," she moaned, with an intensity of ardor that outdid the force of the gale raging outside.

She felt possessed. Her arms flew up around his neck. She stood up on tiptoe and pushed her mouth against his.

His response was as instantaneous as it was forceful, like the hunger of a magnet for its opposite pole. His mouth strained against hers, his tongue probing greedily beyond her lips. The full length of his body crushed against hers, and she returned his longing pressure with her own. As the great ship plunged ahead through the rough seas, they held each other, swaying together in a delirium of delight.

Sandy found herself thinking that, if she could remain in Ken's arms for an eternity, it still wouldn't be long enough, so great was her need for him. But the ship rolled sharply again, this time from side to side, and they fell away from each other. It was as if Neptune, the very god of the sea himself, was determined to tear them apart.

Was that the wind howling outside? Sandy wondered. Or was it the sound of her own fiery blood rushing in her ears?

Sandy stood, bare legs braced and knees slightly bent for support, gazing wide-eyed into Ken's dark and stormy visage. Her bosom still heaved, and her breath still came in light pants. She was painfully aware of the aching wants in her own body.

Then the words that Ken had spoken—could it have

possibly been just moments ago?—again sounded in her mind. *A year,* he had said, *since your husband died. That young man is an actor, and naturally that would make him very attractive to the opposite sex. So what could be more natural . . .*

In a way he was right—not about her attraction to Miles, which was nonexistent. But, she suddenly realized, sooner or later she was going to have to face up to her own needs and how long it had been since she had fulfilled them. Still staring into his eyes, Sandy felt desire wash over her like one of the waves battering against the ship.

But it was too soon. Much too soon to betray the feelings she carried for Philly, the memories of their many years together, which were the backbone of her life. A year might sound like a long time to Ken, who probably never went for more than a few days without a woman in his arms. But to Sandy, the year since Philly had died seemed like no time at all. At least, usually it did.

Looking back into Ken's eyes, her knees felt suddenly weak. She seemed to be dissolving. Sandy didn't want to put a name to the feelings that threatened to engulf her and, shivering, she pulled her robe around her and forced herself to come to her senses.

What was she doing here, half-dressed in the presence of this infamous playboy who collected women the way others collect seashells or postage stamps? Casual sex was not what she needed, and the chances of having any sort of deep relationship with woman-crazy Ken Rexford seemed about zero.

She was on an assignment. There could be no place for passion in this relationship. She looked away from his bare torso. "This should never have happened, Ken," she whispered. "I'm sorry."

He stepped back from her briskly. "No," he said, "it certainly shouldn't have. You were probably frightened by the storm and needed strong arms to protect you. Your great skills at protecting others don't seem to work for yourself. Shall I have the steward page the young actor, bring him back to keep you safe until the seas are calm again?"

He pulled his bathrobe tightly around himself and fastened his eyes, which were filled with bitterness, on her upturned face.

Sandy was silent, reeling with hurt. "Well, perhaps bodyguards aren't trained to cope with the elements," Ken went on. "Only with rude dinner guests and the like. You'd better put something warmer on," he added in an acid undertone and turned quickly away from her. Before Sandy could say anything, two long strides carried him to the door of his stateroom, and in a moment he was gone.

Standing alone, cold and shivering, in the center of the large sitting room, Sandy felt as if her heart had somehow sunk to the bottom of the sea.

7

AMELIA DIDN'T FULLY recover from her bad bout of *mal de mer* until three days after the violent mid-ocean storm had ended. By then the *Voyager Queen* was already nearing Honolulu, and the damage already had been done.

Sandy was all too aware that Ken had been avoiding her since their encounter in her stateroom. Her assignment required her to be at his side during all public occasions, but these were few and far between on board ship.

In fact, Ken had managed to avoid the public entirely. He had sent his young aide, Harvey, to tell her that the time at sea until Honolulu would be spent in a round of political meetings. "The Senator says he'll be taking meals in his stateroom for the next few days," Harvey added, with just the trace of a smirk crossing his face, "so I guess that means your services won't be needed for a while."

Sandy understood how Ken felt. She, too, felt the strain between them that made any but the most circumscribed and formal exchanges embarrassing and painful. She, too, needed time to reflect, so she was glad for the chance to be alone. She had hours to sit on deck and take the sun, to put on her comfortable warmup suit and jog on the ship's promenade deck in the morning, to stand at the rail and gaze out over the vast blue sea. She also caught up on her rest and generally decompressed after the hectic, turbulent beginning of this assignment.

Why was she acting foolishly with Ken? she asked herself again and again. She had always been so sure of herself when it came to self-defense, crowd control, or weapons-and-tactics. And yet, when it came to Ken Rexford, she felt as if she knew nothing at all. Was she totally infatuated with this pompous Casanova? Was she feeling the vast difference in their backgrounds, between her sheltered South Boston upbringing and his wealthy, public one?

She was probably carried away by the *idea* of a man who, though not in office at the moment, held a good deal of political power, not to mention personal and financial clout. Ken was an important man, and everything about him bore this out. What red-blooded woman would not find herself slightly aroused in his presence, Sandy asked herself? After all, he was only about the most attractive looking man alive.

She sighed deeply, aggravated with herself as she gazed out at the flat line of the horizon off the starboard side of the ship. Somehow she felt very small and foolish as she stared out at the vastness of the Pacific Ocean. But not just *anyone* would have been chosen for this assignment, she reminded herself. She could handle Ken Rexford and any of the complications his activities might bring. Whatever she was feeling could be overcome, she told herself, as she tried to convince herself she had taken this assignment *only* for the opportunity of a change of scene and *not* because the first touch of Ken's lips had engraved itself on her mind.

But this pause, this almost carefree breathing time, lasted a few days. When the ship docked in Honolulu the next morning, a whirlwind of activity began.

"We sail again tomorrow at dawn—*sharp*," crusty old Kenneally warned Sandy, as she and Harvey Cattler prepared to follow Ken aboard a small motor launch that would take them to their first Hawaiian appointment.

"No matter what you do, get him back here by then. Understood?"

"Sure, Fitz," Sandy said. "Why aren't you coming?"

"Not enough room in the copter," he growled, "and I hate whirlybirds anyway. Don't forget," he called out as the little boat cast off from the pier, "stay on that schedule."

Wearing the well-hidden shoulder holster that carried her Police Special, Sandy shouldered her leather purse, lifted the canvas overnight bag she had luckily thought to pack, and headed for the gangplank.

She had dreaded seeing Ken, but she needn't have worried. As they boarded the little launch, their eyes never even made contact. She thought perhaps he had nodded vaguely in her direction, but he was talking to members of the delegation who had come out to meet him, and not a word passed between them. Obviously, his anger of the other night was still with him, and he had no intention of acknowledging her presence.

The delegation was something of a surprise to Sandy. Among the white-suited gentlemen who looked obviously Hawaiian were several men dressed in the flowing white burnoose the American public had come to recognize as the national dress of the people of the island of Mauristan. There was a sprinkling of other exotic-looking representatives who might have been from other South Pacific islands, middle eastern and African nations. Sandy felt concerned that no one had bothered to brief her as to exactly who would be present at today's functions—another sign that Ken saw her as totally irrelevant.

But whether or not Ken wanted her along on his little political powwow was beside the point. He was meeting with the public. He would enter crowds, crowds presumably well-filtered and pre-selected by Hawaiian security, but nevertheless, this was when she had to be on her toes. Sandy kept herself posted where she had the best vantage point on Ken. Her eyes scanned the water and the boats around the launch. Sandy O'Hara, bodyguard, was on duty.

If she had needed any reminder of the importance of former U.S. Senator Kenneth Rexford, Sandy got it as soon as the little launch puttered up to the elegantly simple *U.S.S. Arizona* memorial in the center of the calm waters of Pearl Harbor. There, on the white stone span traversing the visible remnant of the U. S. battleship sunk in the World War II attack on Pearl Harbor, stood rows of uniformed officers of the U. S. armed forces, evidently pulled in from bases on the Hawaiian islands to welcome Ken. The Governor of Hawaii was there, surrounded by many white-suited dignitaries of the 50th state, and he greeted Ken warmly.

The usual flashes of electronic strobes Sandy was used to seeing at ceremonies of this sort were conspicuously absent. She noticed this particularly since the lights were always leaving spots before her eyes, making it difficult to observe the goings on in the way she needed to. She wondered if someone had somehow managed to prohibit press coverage. As far as she could tell, there wasn't a reporter in sight.

Now the solemn ceremony began, in which Ken presented a brand-new U. S. flag to the Naval Commander, while the Governor of Hawaii and the state's two senators stood by watching solemnly.

While Harvey remained discreetly in the background, Sandy positioned herself again where she had Ken in full view. She kept her eyes moving back and forth over the people gathered for his talk, while Ken spoke: ". . . from the President himself . . . to fly here at this sacred memorial . . . a new flag to usher in the new year . . . let us never forget . . ."

Suddenly Sandy saw a flash of sun on metal just behind and to the right of Ken. A small gun in a hand extending from under white cotton was pointing toward Ken's head!

Sandy's hand went automatically to her own gun inside her jacket. At just that moment, Ken concluded his remarks and stepped forward to swelling applause on all sides of him.

Sandy dove through the row of people in front of her, her eyes on the flowing white burnoose, which now was still. She threw herself toward the man, her arms outstretched, and caught him behind the knees, sending him in a forward fall to the ground. She reached toward his sleeve, grabbed his gun, and, pointing it skyward, handed it over to one of the Hawaiian policemen, who had evidently seen what she had.

Immediately the crowd gathered around them. Harvey had caught the man's hands and was pinioning him down. Others were gasping, "What is it? What happened?" And Ken was there, staring down at her as she straddled the man, whose angry face snarled up at him and who spat out his words in a strange accent. "You . . . you . . ." he said. "I would have gotten you if it hadn't been for *her* . . . No right you have to meddle in affairs of others . . ."

The loud sound of blowing boat whistles cut him off. Officers of the Coast Guard who had been standing watch in boats around the memorial clattered aboard, and soon Sandy turned her captive over to them. They handcuffed the man, and four of them flanked him and led him off. Through it all, Ken just stood there.

"Someone you know, Senator?" Sandy asked him, smiling confidently as she brushed off her black suit and pushed her flaxen hair out of her face.

The color was returning to Ken's cheeks. "I don't think I've seen *him* before, but I know some of his Mauristanian countrymen." He turned to Sandy and smiled. "Well, I guess you can function without your broom closet and tablecloth after all."

How could he make light of an incident that had just threatened his life? Sandy wondered. How could he show no appreciation of the fact that she had just risked her own life to save him? She had known she didn't understand this man, but now she was sure she never would.

She stepped back to let the Governor, various aides, and members of the delegation surround Ken. They were full of apologies, particularly the other delegates from Mauristan, who seemed aghast at what had happened, or nearly happened. Sandy followed on the edges of the cluster of people around Ken. He was scheduled to go now to a private breakfast with these people, hosted by the Naval Commander.

When they arrived in Honolulu at the official building that had been designated for the meeting, Sandy insisted on checking out the dining room that was set up for the event. She did a thorough check of the room—under tables, behind curtains. She looked in adjoining closets, halls, and rooms. She even insisted on taking a look into the kitchen, where a staff of ten and an equal number of white-uniformed waiters stood prepared to serve the dignitaries.

Explaining who she was and why it was necessary, Sandy frisked each waiter. She sent Harvey to the Governor's top aide for information on all kitchen personnel. It turned out that the chef and his staff were the Governor's private kitchen help, and he personally guaranteed their reliability.

When she was sure all was well and Hawaiian police were posted at all entrances to the room, she sat down with Harvey in a separate anteroom, which guarded the main entrance to the dining room. Ken had gone in this door and would come out of it. Other aides, assistants, and adjutants took nearby tables.

"Well, that was a close one," Harvey said, raising his coffee cup in Sandy's direction. "Here's to one sharp bodyguard!"

"I thought the Senator didn't really need protection on this relaxed pleasure cruise," Sandy replied, smiling.

"It is *mostly* a pleasure cruise," Harvey answered. "But there are some things going on. You'd do best just to keep your eyes peeled at all times."

Changing the subject rapidly, Harvey asked, "What did you think of the Senator's speech?" He barely paused between forkfuls of scrambled eggs and loud slurps of coffee. "Wrote it myself," he said, without waiting for an answer.

"Nice," Sandy said, without much conviction. She took a small sip of fresh orange juice.

"Yeah, I know what you mean," Harvey agreed quickly. "Heard one political speech, you've heard them all." He gave her a sly look through his thick glasses. "Say, you really look sharp this morning. Nice black suit, fancy white blouse, hair all nice and neat. How can you look so pulled together after what you've been through already this morning?"

Sandy had taken a moment to run a comb through her hair before she got off the launch, and if she looked "pulled together" maybe it was because she was feeling the best she had since the trip had begun. This morning's incident had made her feel professional, on-the-job again, and it felt good.

Before she had a chance to answer, Harvey continued, holding a pointed piece of toast in his hand. "Say, what do you call that dress thing?" he asked, pointing to her skirt.

"You mean my culottes?" Sandy asked.

"Yeah, that's it. Culottes. Very flattering, very attractive," Harvey enthused through a mouthful of food.

"Thanks," Sandy said, deciding not to explain that luckily, she had chosen the culottes, and even the flat black shoes she had on, so that her clothing wouldn't hinder her in case fast movement was required. She also didn't mention the Police Special under her jacket, which she had thought for a moment she might have to use. "Thanks for the compliment, Harvey," she said.

Mercifully, the breakfast meeting only lasted two hours. Aides and officials surrounded Ken and the Governor protectively as they moved toward cars assembled in front of the building for the quick motorcade to the nearby military airfield.

In the lead limousine, Ken was flanked by Hawaiian police. Sandy felt at ease taking a seat in the car just behind Ken's, from which she scanned the passing curb-side crowds, as well as the roofs and buildings going by.

When they arrived at the nearby military airfield to which they were going, Ken bade a formal farewell to the Governor and the delegates. The Governor was again full of apologies and embarrassment over the "incident" on the memorial. But Ken, relaxed and smiling, seemed to have all but forgotten his momentary brush with danger. He, Sandy, and Harvey boarded the waiting jet helicopter for the next phase of their Hawaiian journey.

Sandy knew from Kenneally's briefing that this part of their side trip was strictly in connection with Ken's family business interests, and that Amelia had intended to be the one going until she had taken so sick. She claimed her head was still reeling, though the seas had been calm again for days.

The plan was to make the hop over to Kauai, the most northwesterly of the major islands, where Ken wanted to scout locations for a resort hotel that the family was contemplating building. Then they would stay the night in one of the luxurious resorts that already dotted the little island, awaken two hours before sunrise, and rush back to Honolulu in the helicopter to rejoin the cruise ship.

Because of the helicopter's noisy jets, they all wore headphones. Private conversations were impossible any-way—anything spoken into the headset microphones could be heard by all aboard—so Sandy spent the short copter ride looking at the magnificent oceanscapes, while in the seat ahead of her Ken studied his briefing books and, next to her, Harvey dozed.

Now that the group was down to just the three of them plus the pilot, Sandy could let her professional vigil go. She relaxed for the first time that day. Ken was probably so used to Secret Service protection from his days as a senator-in-office, he had probably taken her actions for granted. And why not? She had only been doing her job, after all.

Well, even if Ken Rexford didn't appreciate her swift action today, Philly would have been proud of her, Sandy knew. He had always complimented her prowess as a Secret Service officer.

Idly, Sandy wondered, had it been up to her personally, would she have deemed Ken *worth* the risk of injury or possible death? Doubtful, she said to herself, concluding again that Ken Rexford, suave playboy that he was, wasn't really worth much of anything to her—at least, not in the long run.

Nevertheless, it was only propriety, the glorious ocean vistas, and glimpses of the rocky coral atolls dotting the emerald sea that kept Sandy's eyes from being glued to the nape of Ken's neck. His black hair just touched the collar of the white shirt that peeked above his well-tailored, dark pin-striped suit, and somehow the sight was distracting.

Although Sandy had grown up in Southie, the most insular part of Boston, she had lived all her life in the cities of the Northeast corridor, and business trips had taken her to most parts of the U.S.A. but she reacted with bubbling excitement to the exotic names on the cruise ship's itinerary. Kauai! Oahu! Pago Pago! Fiji! Sri Lanka, the Seychelles and Aphros!

These were names out of a grade-school geography lesson, and to Sandy they were all magic. And as Kauai's sharp black cliffs and lush green mountaintops appeared

out of the sea mists ahead, she was certain they had just
discovered paradise.

The copter pilot's voice came crackling over the ear-
phones. "The Garden Isle ahead, sir," he said to Ken,
as the helicopter seemed to skim the tops of the sparkling
waves like some mechanical watersprite. "Where to, sir?"

"Let's have a look at the Na Pali coast first," Ken
replied, "and a glimpse of the interior too. Then set us
down at the Waiohai, please."

The pilot expertly negotiated his craft above isolated
beaches that seemed to glow tropical pink in the golden
light, over deep-green rain forest and a mountain plateau
wreathed in perpetual cloud, before finally setting down
beside a sprawling luxury hotel that rose from behind
palm trees on a pristine beach at the water's edge.

Even before the hotel manager could show them to
their top-floor suites, Ken was eager to go exploring.

"Ready, Harvey?" he asked tersely, adding pointedly,
"And you, *Ms*. O'Hara?" turning directly to Sandy for
the first time that day.

Sandy shrugged noncommittally, but Harvey immediately begged off. "Gee, boss, you know I've got this
foot problem, the one that kept me out of the service.
I'd like to come, but I should really be working on your
Great Wall speech and . . ."

Ken waved off further explanation. "Okay, Harvey,
you're off the hook. Well, how about you, madam bodyguard? After this morning, perhaps you'd like the afternoon off for a little rest, too?" Ken asked, loosening his
tie and taking off his suit jacket, which he handed to the
relieved young aide.

"Not at all, *Senator* Rexford," Sandy replied, matching his tone. "My job is to stay with you, and that's what
I'm here for——to do my job, in case you hadn't noticed."

"Nothing more dangerous on Kauai than falling co-
conuts," he observed acidly. "But have it your way," he
added, striding off across the warm sandy beach. "And

come along if you want." Sandy pointed out her overnight bag to the bellboy, who said he would leave it in her room.

At first Sandy felt a little ridiculous marching across the beach in her dark business suit, following after Ken, who was still wearing his black trousers, white dress shirt, and loosened silk tie. She struggled to keep up, trying to hop along in the footsteps left by his stylish, tassel-topped loafers. But finally she slipped off her own shoes, shoved them into her shoulder bag, and stopped worrying about the effect of the hot sun on her appearance. Soon the years of strenuous physical exercise began to pay off, and she caught up to the tall, hard-striding politician.

It was hard to believe it was the beginning of February, and that only days ago she had raced through a blizzard to catch a plane. It was even harder to believe that only a few hours ago she had felled and straddled a would-be assassin.

Now the warm sun seemed to bake away her cares, and the foamy blue sea lapping at the clean white shoreline, only a few feet away, soothed her frazzled nerves. The heady scent of orchids came wafting to her on a gentle breeze.

Sandy recalled the last several days as she listened to the rustle of the swaying palms and the chattering song of tropical birds.

She sneaked a quick glance up at Ken and was glad to notice the closed, determined look on his face and the perspiration that dotted his furrowed brow. Nature, she thought, was putting things in perspective. See, it seemed to be saying, not all the world is harsh and cruel and dangerous—

Without quite realizing what she was doing, Sandy began to whistle a little tune as she basked in the beauty of the day around her.

Walking beside her, Ken frowned. *"That* certainly is

an appropriate song," he muttered irritably.

Sandy returned his stern glower with a tentative, but puzzled smile. "This place is beautiful," she observed brightly. "It makes me happy to be here. And—and, I'd be even happier if we could maybe bury the hatchet, get back to a first-name basis again, maybe even start over as friends. It is going to be a long—and after today I'd say, strenuous—trip."

Ken was staring straight ahead, off into the forested middle distance. Without slackening his stride, he cleared his throat and mumbled under his breath, "Okay, if that's the way you want it . . . Sandy."

His distant, grudging demeanor was like a blast of arctic wind over the soothing tropical scene. Sandy pulled up short and put her hands on her hips. "Just wait a minute, *Mister* Senator," she called out angrily, but Ken continued striding ahead, and she had to run to catch up with him.

"You have a lot of nerve patronizing me," she sputtered. "If you're still mad about the other night, *who* was it who jumped to conclusions?"

Ken stuck out his chin, hunched up his shoulders, and kept striding on. Sandy stopped dead in her tracks and glared at his retreating back. "And who saved whose life this morning, anyway?" she yelled at the top of her lungs. Startled by the sound, a small covey of red-and-blue birds exploded from the cover of the rain forest ahead.

Just before reaching the end of the pristine white beach, Ken stopped and turned around slowly. "I guess you really are a bodyguard, after all," he said in a soft voice. "You seem to know all kinds of tricks to subdue dangerous men." A slow grin broke over his face.

"I told you, strength is more mental than physical. But Ken, who was he, the man from Mauristan? Why would he want to kill you? What did he mean you shouldn't meddle in others' affairs?" Her questions came all at once.

"I can't tell you much yet, Sandy," he said. "All I can say is that he shouldn't have been cleared as a member of the delegation from North Mauristan."

"Why a delegation from that besieged little island?" she asked.

"Before this trip is over, I hope you'll understand why. You and a lot of other people," Ken answered, a worried frown creasing his brow. "Anyway, the Coast Guard will turn him over to the proper authorities. We won't see that fellow again. But keep up the good work." He crossed the hot sand to where she was standing. "Maybe this is the time to tell you, Sandy. I've changed my mind about female bodyguards."

Sandy smiled up at him and basked for a moment in her victory. "About the other night . . ." she began, wanting to clear the air completely.

"The other night," Ken broke in. "I'm sorry. I did jump to conclusions without giving you a chance to explain. I was offended, you could say, by the sight of you and that actor. And I had no right to be. Let's let bygones be bygones. Fair enough, Sandy?"

Sandy could tell that Ken was being sincere. "Okay, Ken," she said, smiling and shaking his hand solemnly. "Friends."

"Friends," he agreed.

They walked on together into the dense forest, following a narrow trail through the lush undergrowth, and soon Sandy found herself whistling *that* tune again. "I'm gonna dah-dah-dah-dah-DAH-ta-dah-dah," she sang under her breath, trying to remember the words.

Ken stopped in the middle of the trail and took a folded map from his breast pocket. "Let's see, I was sure it was somewhere near here," he said, wiping the perspiration from his forehead with the back of his sleeve. "I think the family land is over that way," he said, pointing to a thick growth of ferns. "It's supposed to be a beautiful spot," he added, putting the map back into his pocket.

"The architects say it would make a great place for a new hotel, but I'm not so sure."

He plunged ahead, pushing the thick ferns aside, and Sandy continued close behind. Once again she whistled the same fragment of song. "What's the title of that, Ken?" she asked lightly, once again feeling as buoyant as the bouncy little tune. "And what did you mean when you said it was appropriate?"

"You mean you actually don't know what you've been singing?" Ken gave her an incredulous look over his shoulder as he pushed his way through thick fronds. "I thought it was a message you were sending me—a statement of your position."

The fragrance of orchids was stronger now, mixing with the rich scent of damp grass. Ken pushed aside the last of the tangled forest undergrowth, and Sandy stepped out beside him to the edge of a little forest glade. At its center was a shimmering pool of crystal-clear blue water, on the calm surface of which floated delicate tropical orchids. Suddenly it came to her: "I'm gonna wash that man right outta my hair." So that was the song she had been humming!

She started to laugh, and Ken looked at her questioningly. "I must feel like Mary Martin in *South Pacific*," she explained. "I've only seen tropical beauty like this in the movies, and that song seems to go with it."

"It certainly is beautiful," Ken answered, sweeping his hand to indicate not only the little sylvan glade and the small, rainbow-flecked waterfall Sandy could just barely glimpse through the thick foliage beyond, but also the beach they had just walked on and the rest of beautiful Kauai as well. "So, you weren't trying to send me a message?" he asked, his back to her as he plopped down abruptly on the thick grass at the edge of the calm pool and began taking off his shoes and socks.

"Well, let's just say it wasn't a *conscious* message," Sandy answered teasingly.

"I think I've been in politics too long," Ken muttered, holding up one scuffed, baby-calf loafer and giving it a good shake so that a stream of sand fell out. He did the same to the other shoe. "I'm getting too suspicious and set in my ways," he pronounced, "*and* taking myself too seriously. But that's what being a public figure does to you," he added.

Sandy sat down next to him on the grassy bank. "Well, no wonder," she said, sympathetically. "You even have to get used to being a target for the guns of crazies. Maybe you should give up politics." She slipped off her black suit jacket and the leather shoulder holster under it and laid them with her shoulder bag on the grass behind her.

"Actually I'll know more about my future when this trip is over," Ken said, his features tightening. "But this is no place to talk about careers."

Sandy leaned over and smiled at her reflection in the clear waters of the calm pool. "No," she agreed.

They seemed to be talking together like two friendly human beings. This was more like it, she thought. Perhaps they could get to know each other better today. She sensed a vulnerability and boyishness in Ken that she had suspected were there, just under the smooth, ultra-refined surface, but which she had not seen before. Beside her, as if to confirm her warm feelings, Ken dipped his big toe into the water, sending little waves radiating through the shimmering reflection.

"Why don't we rest here awhile before going back," he suggested. He leaned back and stretched out on the soft grass with his legs crossed and his hands behind his head. "It's so peaceful," he murmured.

"Look!" he called out suddenly, stabbing a finger toward the sky. Quickly, Sandy glanced up to where he was pointing. Two streaks of bright yellow and deep blue were chasing each other from branch to branch across the bright patch of blue sky above the small glade.

"Birds," Sandy said delightedly, leaning back and stretching out next to him. "A pair of beautiful birds. What kind do you suppose they are?"

"I don't know," Ken replied. "Ornithology was never my strong suit."

Lying next to him and feeling the pleasure of this idle moment, Sandy chuckled. "Why, I thought you political fellows have to know everything about *everything* before you run the country," she needled good-naturedly. "Isn't that what you tell the voters?"

Ken's amused laugh sent the colorful birds diving for the cover of a tall palm frond. "Yes, yes, that *is* true," he said in a self-mocking voice. "We *do* know everything about everything. Now let's see. What *were* those birds?"

Sandy smiled and watched his handsome features pull into a contemplative scowl, his eyebrows raised high. "I've got it," he continued in the same deep orator's voice. "Those birds were tropical lovebirds. Yes, that's it. A rare species of bird indeed, the seldom seen Blue and Gold Streaked Lovebird." He pulled himself up on one elbow and gave her a crooked grin.

"I find your erudition overwhelming, sir," Sandy said in a tone of high sophistication, which apparently Ken found a challenge. He stared silently in her direction and then said in a new tone of voice, "Sandy, stay still. Don't move."

She froze as Ken turned toward her, one arm raised. With a sudden sweep downward and across her shoulder, he removed some small living creature from her person. Sandy began to giggle.

"Have you just saved *my* life?" she asked, grinning broadly at him.

"The world is now populated by one less small black spider," he said, giving her a beam of overstated pride. He was sitting very close to her. A wicked look crossed his handsome features. "I just realized—I bet you're ticklish!"

"No! You wouldn't dare!"

"Oh, wouldn't I?"

In a flash he was up, his knees straddling her torso and pinning her to the soft ground. His fingers danced up and down the sides of her rib cage, and Sandy squirmed and bucked and giggled and laughed.

"No, no, no, no, *no!* Stop, stop, *stop!*" She slapped playfully at his hands, but he grabbed her wrists and pinned them under his knees.

"Say 'uncle,'" he demanded.

Sandy shook her head furiously from side to side and thrust her hips up suddenly, trying to buck him off. But she was too weak from laughter, and all she managed to do was to push his body forward and down, so that his head was inches from her own.

"I'll bet your neck's ticklish too," he announced gleefully, thrusting his patrician nose into the little hollow formed where the base of her long neck met her shoulder bone.

"Ah! Ah!" Sandy squealed, writhing and twisting with renewed force. "You are torturing me, Ken . . . please . . ."

"I knew it!" he cried triumphantly. "I've found your weak spot, your window of vulnerability!"

"Please, please stop," Sandy begged, gasping for breath, snickering and scrunching up her shoulders at the same time. "Uncle, uncle—I'll say anything you want!"

"Too late," Ken retorted.

Sandy felt something warm and wet burrowing into her ear. She hunched up her shoulders and shivered with surprise at the exquisitely tingling touch of his tongue. The scent of tropical blossoms that had filled her nostrils was overwhelmed by the sharp sandalwood musk of *eau de cologne*.

Her convulsive gasps were turning into ragged, panting breaths, and the sharp, evasive squirms became the sinuous churning of her hips.

He ran his tongue around the outer whorls of her ear.

He took the lobe in his teeth and nibbled it gently before flicking his tongue up and down and up and down her long, straining neck. The quickening puffs of his breath turned to hot fire against her skin.

He kissed her—her chin, her closed eyes, the tip of her nose. His fiery tongue probed between her moist, bowed lips.

He stretched out—slowly, slowly—his body rubbing sensuously against hers. And her hands, like love birds, flew around him—tangling in his hair, stroking his neck, running up and down his taut spine—always pressing him closer and closer to her.

Urgently, he fumbled at the buttons of her blouse, unfastening them one by one, until it was completely open. The lacy, low-cut French bra she wore underneath unsnapped in the front, and in an instant it was unhooked.

His kisses rained down on her bare throat, her chest, the firm twin mounds of her exposed breasts.

He raised his head and kissed her lips again—hard, savagely hard, with all the explosive force of long-checked passion suddenly released.

His hand traced the outline of her straining breasts and stroked lightly around their taut tips. It ran down and down, over her undulating belly, to the edge of her culottes. He undid the narrow belt. His hand found the hidden side zipper. Slowly, he began to pull it down.

"Wait!" She held his hand firmly with her own. "Please wait."

"What? What is it, Sandy?" He raised his head, then bent forward to kiss her again, but her hand against his chest stopped him.

"I—I—" she panted, gasping to take in more air. She looked up at him through long lashes, from eyes half-closed in ecstasy. Her lips quivered as she spoke. "There's so much misunderstanding between us. I—I still don't know why you kissed me back then—so long ago . . . I still haven't explained Miles . . ."

He laughed. "It's so simple, Sandy, but now's not the time," he murmured. "None of those things matter, believe me..."

Only the pressure of her hand kept him from immediately kissing her. "The other night—what you thought then—it isn't true, but you don't know it. There's so much misunderstanding," she repeated in a pleading voice. "So much left unsaid..."

"I know, I know," he said soothingly. "But I trust you, I do, just as you'll have to trust me."

Hesitantly, hopefully, she nodded her agreement.

His dark eyes seemed to stare deeply into hers. "Only one thing matters, only one thing that I can say." He inclined his head toward her until his lips brushed her ear. "I want you," he whispered. "I want you, Sandy O'Hara..."

Somewhere a bird song sounded, somewhere a sea breeze blew. But she heard nothing but his whispered endearments, felt nothing but the hot touch of his hand, tasted nothing but his salty lips.

He pulled off her culottes. His fingers were butterflies dancing down her long legs as he rolled down her pantyhose, leg by leg.

In another frenzy of passion he nearly tore off her filmy white panties before she was able to raise her knees and push up her hips to help him along.

She lay naked on the matted ground, a forearm thrown over her fevered brow, watching as he pulled off his clothes in a furiously eager transport of excitement. Not once did he take his eyes off her unclothed form.

And then at last—under the deep blue sky and beside the clear waters of the peaceful pool—they made love. Their naked bodies embraced and entwined, pulled apart and drew together again. Over and over again he whispered her name, and over and over again his hungry lips feasted on her burning skin.

She wrapped herself around him and dug her hands

into the hard muscles of his back and buried her head in his strong chest. She cried out with pleasure—again and again.

When they were both spent, and she was cradled in his arms, looking up at the azure sky and at the wet, emerald leaves of the tropical grove all around, Sandy felt as if she were seeing everything for the first time. The whole world had a fresh and crystal clarity that brought tears of joy to her eyes.

Finally they fell asleep, until they were awakened by the buzz of a passing aircraft. Then they whispered foolish endearments to each other. They touched lovingly and the long day passed.

At last, when the sky had deepened to a glowing sapphire and the first, faint stars were winking in the heavens, and the little glade was dappled by the growing shadows, they got up and dressed. Slowly, reluctantly, they walked hand in hand through the damp rain forest and along the narrow beach toward the golden lights of the deluxe resort hotel where they were to spend the night.

8

IN MANY WAYS the fancy Hanalei Room restaurant on the elegant hotel's top floor reminded Sandy of the cruise ship's ballroom. There was the same well-set table, the crisp linen tablecloth a perfect match for the fine china, with gleaming silverware reflecting the burnished glow of the subdued candlelight that flickered from above the graceful floral arrangement at the table's center. There were the same quietly attentive, red-jacketed waiters anticipating their every need. And there were the rich furnishings, the fine art works and the luxuriantly growing potted plants. There was even a spectacular sea view.

But most important, there was Ken, wearing a tuxedo and gazing raptly into her eyes. When they had come in from their tryst, Sandy had bathed and changed into a beaded, apricot silk-organza chemise, another of her Washington purchases. It had a daringly decolleté neckline, and she was glad she'd thought to fold it into her small overnight bag. She didn't need the appreciative stares of the other men dining in the restaurant, or Harvey's bug-eyed greeting when she appeared at the table, to tell her how she looked in the shimmering, clinging dress. Ken's look was testimony enough!

Sandy ordered dinner and the courses came and went, but she was unable to eat much of anything.

"Was the food not to madam's satisfaction?" The waiter's solicitous question, as he paused before whisking away her plate of untouched *mahi mahi*, momentarily broke the invisible electric spark that was arcing across the table between her and Ken.

"I just wasn't hungry," Sandy said softly, glancing up and favoring the waiter with a small smile. "Thank you." She decided not to mention that it was impossible for her to have even a single bite of dolphin once she realized that that was what *mahi mahi* was.

Her eyes flicked from the disappearing waiter to Harvey, the third person at their little table, who was seated midway between her and Ken. For some reason, she had uncharacteristically followed Harvey's suggestion to "try some of the delicious *mahi*" without question. Perhaps it was simply the perfection of the night, she thought. Or rather the perfection of the afternoon, she added to herself, letting an enigmatic smile cross her features. Her gaze swept back across the table to Ken's handsome face, and their eyes locked once again in unspoken communion. Vaguely, she was aware that Harvey was *still* talking, barely pausing to chew his prodigious bites of food. But then again, Harvey had been jabbering away throughout dinner.

"...so I got worried, wondering where you'd gotten to. It's still a big jungle out there, and I knew Fitz would break my leg if anything went wrong, so I took a walk out on the beach. It's really nice out there, you know, and not at all as deserted as you'd think. There's a bunch of really nice hotels out here already. A Sheraton even, and this fancy converted sugar plantation. Anyway, I was worried when I still didn't find you, so you know what I did?" Harvey paused to gulp down a large swallow of *Nozzole Bianco*. "You're going to laugh," he added, chuckling to himself.

He looked from Ken to Sandy and back again. "Hey, you okay?" he asked, his round, owlish face furrowing in a frown. "You two haven't said a dozen words between you since dinner started."

Ken's hand had been moving slowly across the table,

idly toying with his butter knife, reaching out for the glass pepper shaker, caressing the stem of his wine glass. Now he withdrew the hand, turned slowly toward his talkative assistant, and gave him a distant, neutral stare. "Everything's fine, Harvey," he said in a voice whose quietly authoritative tone brooked no questioning. "It's just been a long day. So, tell us, what did you do that we're going to find so amusing?"

"I called the copter to go looking for you, is what I did," Harvey replied with a snicker. "You know how I hate to fly, boss. That's how worried I was . . ."

"Really?" Ken interjected smoothly, arching an eyebrow quizzically. "And was your helicopter trip uneventful?"

"Weelll . . ." Harvey began insinuatingly. He looked from side to side, leaned forward, and whispered conspiratorially, "I don't exactly know how to put this," he said, licking his lips, "without being indelicate about it, but we buzzed this little clearing in the forest where there was this couple, you see, and they were, ah, 'in the act,' if you know what I mean. How shall I put it?—*in flagrante delicto* is the expression, I believe."

Sandy saw Ken stiffen instantly, his eyes narrowing and his lips pursed in a tight line. Her own cheeks, she could feel, were flushing red with embarrassment. Fortunately, Harvey was too preoccupied by his memory of the sight to notice.

"I couldn't believe it. A sight like that right out there in the middle of the jungle! Well, here's the funniest thing. You know what I thought at first?" Harvey paused for dramatic effect. "I thought it was the two of you! Why, I even told the copter pilot to turn around and make another pass, but he was too low on fuel by then and we had to come back."

"I'm not amused," Ken said coldly. "That's not the kind of story you repeat in front of a lady. I think you owe Ms. O'Hara an apology."

Sandy was about to protest, to say it wasn't necessary, but the words froze in her throat. She was shocked to think that, while she and Ken had been transported to what they'd thought was their own private world of bliss, they had been seen—and laughed at—from a helicopter. Now she was doubly shocked to feel a foot running up and down her stockinged leg. Could Ken be this carelessly brazen? she wondered incredulously, her eyes widening with surprise.

"I'm sorry," Harvey said meekly, looking down at the table. "I meant no disrespect. Just thought you'd be amused."

"No offense taken," Sandy replied quickly, uncomfortably aware of the foot rubbing along her calf. "A closed issue as far as I'm concerned."

"Good," Ken said gruffly. "I'm going up to get some rest. May I escort you to your room, Ms. O'Hara?" he asked pointedly, his eyes blazing momentarily with desire.

Sandy realized instantly that Ken's question was really an invitation. But she knew that if she went with him at that moment there would be no denying his passionate needs—nor would she want to. It seemed wiser not to add to Harvey's suspicions or to risk the suspicions of others in the hotel. If the press picked up the idea that she and Ken were lovers, the consequences could be disastrous, at least for her. Ken was used to scandal, but it would certainly be the end of her career.

"Thank you, Senator. I think I'll stay a moment and finish my coffee," she replied quietly, hoping he would understand.

"Me too, boss," Harvey agreed immediately.

A strange look passed over Ken's face. Perhaps he was even more jolted than she by the thought that his aides had seen them from the sky. Perhaps he was misinterpreting her reasons for staying behind now with Harvey. It was more than Sandy could sort out, and before she could think of anything to say to smooth things over, Ken was glaring at her and giving a hostile shrug. "Suit yourselves," he said tersely. "Remember we're leaving awfully early in the morning to return to the ship." Then, without looking at Sandy, he stood and strode magistrally from the dining room.

And it was then that Sandy received another shock. The stroking pressure on her leg continued!

She fixed Harvey with a murderous glare as she instantly slid her chair back from the table and away from his offending foot. "If you ever dare to do that again, you presumptuous clod, I'll break *both* your legs," she hissed furiously. "And that's just for starters. Do you understand?"

"Weelll . . ." Before he could reply, Sandy was up and striding imperially from the room, leaving the amorous aide in mid-sentence talking to an empty chair.

Sandy knocked on Ken's door, gently at first and then harder. But there was no answer. She wanted to find him, to know how he felt about Harvey's news, to straighten things out, but he was nowhere to be found. So she went to her room.

She was unable to sleep a wink all night, thinking about the distressing implications of what had happened and what Ken's crass political aide had said.

Of course Harvey knew! Or at least he suspected strongly, she realized, and that was why he had dared to play footsie under the table with her at dinner. The very thought of his despicable presumption brought her angry indignation boiling to the surface each time she thought of it. She wished she had slapped his smirking face right on the spot!

But, on further reflection, she felt she had only herself to blame. *How* could she have given in to her passion like that? *How* could she have failed to see the terrible dangers ahead?

That she had fallen madly in love with Ken Rexford
was no excuse. She should have remembered she was a
young widow, unused to the attentions of men. She should
have remembered how, after Philly's untimely death, she
had told herself time and again that there would be no
second man, no second love, for her. After all, hadn't
she vowed to herself never to depend upon—much less
fall for—any man again?

What must Ken think of her? Surely, she was just
another in the long line of his many conquests. Wasn't
that his reputation anyway? *Senator Ken Rexford, the
Playboy Politician*...How could she have disregarded
that?

It was too late to do anything now to make amends,
she realized with some chagrin. She would have to learn
this hard lesson and bear her shame without complaint.
But once the ship reached Australia, she would demand
to be taken off the assignment, to be replaced by someone
who wouldn't make the mistake of getting emotionally
involved. A man—a man would have been better for
this job after all.

The long night passed. Once, while she was pacing
the hotel room, worrying through her apprehensions and
coming to her fateful decision, there was a knock on her
door. At first, forgetting everything, she wanted to rush
over and open it and throw herself into Ken's arms. But
she looked at the clock—it was nearly two in the morning—and remembered the frosty expression on his face
when he had left the dinner table so abruptly.

What if it wasn't him? What if it was his despicable
aide, bringing champagne and innuendo? She forced herself to stand quietly and wait and listen. She didn't open
the door or acknowledge the knock when it was repeated
or move a muscle when the unknown person in the hall
tried the door knob and found it was locked. After several
minutes, while she remained motionless on one side of
the closed door, sensing that the person in the hallway

was doing the same, she heard the sound of muffled footsteps receding.

At last, in the eerie predawn darkness, Sandy, Ken, and Harvey met in the empty lobby. Ken grumbled a "Good morning" to the two of them, and successfully avoided meeting Sandy's eyes. They left the hotel in mutual silence and boarded the waiting jet helicopter for the quick flight across the waters to Honolulu and the departing cruise ship.

Sandy welcomed the darkness outside and the noise of the helicopter's jets, which prevented talk or even thought. While the copter raced the dawn back to Oahu, she sat in the back of the craft's small cabin and slept.

They made it back to the *Voyager Queen* with only moments to spare before the giant luxury liner steamed out of the harbor. But there was no time to stand at the stern rail and watch the lovely Hawaiian island recede. As soon as they were aboard, they were met by Amelia and Fitzpatrick Kenneally, who both looked deeply worried.

"Get a load of this," Ken's chief political aide growled, pushing a piece of paper into Ken's hand.

Ken quickly scanned the words on the paper. When he looked up, his face was set in an expression of granite hardness.

Unexpectedly, he turned to Sandy. In a strained, almost choked voice, he asked her, "Did you call the ship last night from the hotel?"

Sandy realized that Amelia and Fitz were watching her with concern on their faces. "No, I didn't. I didn't call anywhere. Why..."

"A little publicity to help you along on your way to Hollywood?" Ken snapped cruelly, abruptly turning his attention to Harvey, who was standing quietly in the background. "Harvey? Did you?"

"I went straight to bed after dinner," the young assistant said emphatically.

Ken's quick glance back in Sandy's direction was sharp and probing. Then he looked away from her again, down at the deck. "And what do you say?" he asked. "Did you make any phone calls from anywhere on the island of Kauai last night to the ship, or to anywhere in Honolulu?"

"No," Sandy said. "But I still don't see..." Looking at her, Ken's face twisted in rage as he crumpled the piece of paper in his hand. "Here," he said bitterly, giving it to Sandy. "This should explain. C'mon Fitz, you too Harvey, we've got a lot of damage-control planning to do," he added. "It does seem odd that I can keep the press away from a meeting of hundreds in Hawaii and can't keep this sort of thing out of the headlines."

"I may have some ideas on how we should approach this, boss," Harvey was saying, as Ken turned on his heel and marched away, his two aides following closely behind.

"What is all this?" Sandy asked Amelia, who was left standing with her on the deck.

"It's the text of a long radio telegram, sent from the ship late last night by Babs Teller," Amelia said, as Sandy unfolded the crumpled paper.

"Babs Teller? Oh, the television gossip columnist..."

"She's got a syndicated newspaper column, too," Amelia said ominously. "That's the text of her next column. It'll be appearing by tonight in about a thousand newspapers."

"But how did you get it?" Sandy asked.

Amelia looked all around, and then said in a whisper, "The Captain gave it to me in strictest confidence. He's been coming up to visit me ever since I was seasick. Needless to say, he's been a dear. Showing me that cable was a violation of all the rules, he said, but he told me he just had to do it. He also said Babs got a radio-

telephone call from Kauai just before she sent out this
cable."

"Oh?" Sandy replied diffidently, beginning to read
the text of the cablegram. As she read, her unconcern
gave way to horror. "Good lord!" she gasped. "This is
all about me!"

She could barely believe the words she was reading.

*—SENATOR AND MYSTERY WOMAN IN
TROPICAL TRYST—What California politician on
a luxurious 'round-the-world cruise just spent a
romantic afternooon and evening alone with a mysterious blonde bombshell, torridly romancing her
on a beautiful island in Hawaii? (Hint: he's Washington's most eligible bachelor.) My shipboard spy
says she's a bodyguard of all things, assigned by
the private Exec Protective Agency, a respected
security-for-hire outfit headquartered in McLean,
Va . . .*

*But the real question on everyone's lips is: Who's
guarding whose body, and why? I can only tell you
this, dear readers. With her movie-star looks and
bod to match, our Senator better watch out! He
better guard his bodyguard's beautiful bod better,
and he better take careful note of her intense interest in a sexy young actor who's also on board!*

*Could it be that our Senator's latest fling is the
most serious yet? And could it be that his sexy
young female bodyguard is turning the tables on
him? Is it executive protection or true love that
she's pursuing? Or maybe our young actor is filling
her pretty head with thoughts of Hollywood and
an acting career?*

*Watch this space for more news on the most
glamorous Hollywood-Potomac love triangle of the
year . . .*

"Oh no! How can this be?" Sandy felt stricken. Each word of the terrible gossip column was a dagger, pricking her heart and puncturing her fragile self-esteem. She looked up at Amelia. "How can this be?" she repeated in a pleading voice. "Do you think Ken doesn't believe me, Amelia? Surely he doesn't believe that I'm interested in an acting career just because Miles Moore thinks I *should* be."

Amelia put a consoling arm around Sandy's shoulder. "I don't know what Ken thinks, but I don't think he would judge anyone without proof, and I don't think he'll find any where you're concerned. You have to understand that Ken has had many bad experiences with gold-digging women, Sandy. Believe me, more than one has tried to use him for a little free publicity. But let him cool off. If my brother isn't a good enough judge of people to figure out—"

"I am going to resign, Amelia," Sandy interrupted with determination. "I was already thinking of it. I could tell that this wasn't working out, that I wasn't any help."

"No! Don't you do it!" Amelia insisted. "I know something else I'm not supposed to. And the press hasn't got this. The Captain received news from the Hawaiian police about the incident at Ken's speech. I know you saved his life, Sandy. Now you see that he really does need you on this trip, that there are certain factions who would just as soon his mission fail."

"Why does everyone know about this mission except me? I'm the one expected to deal with the dangers, and I haven't any idea what's going on, Amelia."

"I know. Ken can't tell anyone the full story yet. I only know part of it myself. Just believe in him, Sandy. I do."

"The way he believes in me?" she asked. "He actually thinks I gave that story to the press."

"Well, I'm sure you didn't. None of this is *your* fault. You can't keep people from talking or jumping to their own conclusions. But you *can* continue to do your job. Eventually they'll see they were wrong in their hasty judgments, dear. And that includes Kenny."

Time was something there was plenty of on board the *Voyager Queen,* Sandy discovered as she fell into the unhurried rhythm of shipboard life. The stately liner made its progress South and West, crossing first the International Date Line and then the equator as it navigated the warm seas.

The days were sunny and bright, and the vast blue ocean was calm and sparkling. Each pure, clear day passed smoothly into a luminous, starry night. Warm sea breezes played over gentle ocean swells.

Again, Ken spent his days closeted with his two assistants, immersed in the mysterious strategy sessions of his "mission," Sandy supposed. She felt her hackles rise every time she thought of the secret goings on around her. If that first day in the Capitol building had had to do with Ken's current undertakings, and he had said as much, then she had been involved from Day One. As a bodyguard offering protection to someone involved in possible life-threatening situations, she felt she should have been briefed on the real nature of her job.

But Ken hadn't taken her into his confidence—on anything. Since the day on Kauai they had never seen each other alone, had not had a conversation to unravel the tension resulting from the events that had followed. While he was working in his stateroom, she was again free to think quietly.

Between now and docking on the island of Fiji, Sandy would have to decide whether or not to stay on as Ken's bodyguard. The question haunted her, and she swung back and forth between feeling a duty to stay, and feeling that, by falling in love with him, she had disqualified herself as a suitable employee on his staff.

She was letting the problem drift, trying not to focus

on it. Sometimes she came up with answers that way. She kept busy, dividing her days among the many activities aboard ship. Amelia wasn't around very much since she was taking care to be available for any free time Captain McCabe could find. So Sandy created a routine for herself, a program that attempted to push Ken's aristocratic visage, and especially the passion-filled look she had seen in his eyes on the island, out of her thoughts.

Each morning she ran twenty-five times around the Promenade Deck, then went below for a sauna or a massage. She explored the ship's many decks, browsing in its boutiques, sipping coffee in its cafes, or strolling around its miles of corridors.

Each afternoon she went to the gym and worked out. For ninety minutes she put herself through the complex and graceful movements of the martial arts. Then she headed for the outdoor swimming pool, near the stern on the Lower Promenade, where she would do laps until she was utterly exhausted. Then she either sat in the late-afternoon sun or returned to her room to prepare for the formal evening dinners.

At first, she had added marksmanship practice to her daily regimen, spending an hour each afternoon with a small rifle at the stern shooting traps. Her hand was steady and her aim was true. Clay pigeon after clay pigeon fell shattered into the ship's wake. Reports of her marksmanship circulated quickly, and each new day brought a larger crowd of applauding, admiring gawkers. On the third day, when she saw harsh Mr. Hartmann in the crowd with a drink in his hand and Babs Teller watching her from behind big, dark sunglasses, Sandy gave up the trapshooting.

She also checked the ship's schedule, posted every morning on a bulletin board in the Purser's Lounge, to find out where the film company was shooting that day. Then she would make certain to avoid that part of the ship. She had already had enough embarrassment for *ten* around-the-world cruises, she decided, so it was worth avoiding Miles and his Hollywood crew. If she was seen with them, Ken would be sure to hear about it, and his suspicions about her secret wish for a movie career or about whatever he thought her relationship with Miles was would only be confirmed in his mind.

Once, going out of her way to avoid the film company after her midday swim, Sandy found herself in an unfamiliar part of the Veranda Deck. She wore a short, white terrycloth beach jacket over a skimpy red bandeau bikini. Her shaggy blond locks were still dripping wet. She ducked into a small, dark lounge to contemplate the quickest way to her cabin when, to her surprise, she found Amelia and Fitzpatrick Kenneally there, sitting at the bar and talking as they sipped icy drinks.

"Hi," she said, approaching them gingerly, afraid she might be interrupting their conversation.

"I was here waiting for the Captain," Amelia said brightly, "when I ran into Fitz. Ken finally gave him a few hours off."

"So we're having a few to celebrate my newfound, but no doubt short-lived, freedom," Kenneally remarked. "Would you care to join us, lass?"

"No, no, I couldn't," Sandy said quickly, thinking that the crusty old aide was only being uncharacteristically polite. She pointed to her skimpy bathing suit and wet hair. "I should really get out of these clothes anyway. But thanks."

Kenneally leaned so far forward that for a moment Sandy was afraid he would fall right off the bar stool. Closing one eye, he growled in his whiskey voice, "Come now, girl, you can't turn down a drink during the cocktail hour on board a ship like this! Where's your sense of fun!"

"Besides," he continued, with a nod toward Amelia, "I was just asking where you'd been keeping yourself, how you were getting along and such. It's been so long since we've seen your smilin' face, I thought you might've fallen overboard and drowned," he added with a snort. "It's lucky for us all you didn't, otherwise the Senator would be minus a darn good bodyguard." He gave her a knowing look that led her to believe he also knew about the skirmish in Honolulu harbor. "So come along, girl, and let's all have that drink," he concluded.

Sandy returned his smile. "Well, I don't know..."

"Do join us, Sandy," Amelia interjected. "It'll do us all some good to let our hair down just a little. I'll tell you what, we'll go out, sit in the deck chairs, and have the stewards bring our drinks out there. That way you can sit in the sun and won't have to worry about a chill."

"Well...okay."

Fitz ordered a round of drinks to be sent out to them, and they all trooped outside and settled into three adjoining deck chairs with an unimpeded view of the glittering blue ocean.

Sandy slipped off her beach jacket and stretched out comfortably in the middle chair, a cool *mai tai* in her hand, while on either side of her Amelia and Fitz chattered on about the weather and the beauty of the scenery and the vacation prospects ahead. Though their conversation was only small-talk, Sandy found that she was glad to be there, soaking up sun and the warm feeling that came with being with people again. The conversation had finally turned to Ken, and Fitz was on the verge of answering Amelia's seemingly casual question about how things were going with her brother and his work, when a sudden cloud appeared. The cloud was in the form of a small woman with a big bouffant hair-do and large, dark sunglasses. Her compact body looked as if it would burst with repressed energy.

Standing in front of Sandy so that she blocked the sun, Babs Teller put her tiny hands on her hips. "Well,

well, well, look who's here," she said. "The Mystery Woman herself."

Sandy squinted, trying to make out the face outlined by the corona of the blazing sun. She sat up, shading her eyes with her hand. "We've never been introduced," she said reprovingly. "I'm not any Mystery Woman, you know. If you had taken the time to ask, you would have found *that* much out at least."

"That's assuming you would have talked to me in the first place," the gossip columnist replied with syrupy sweetness. "Surely you see that the story's so much better this way, with my thousands and thousands of readers just *so eager* to learn what comes next.".

"But what you wrote isn't true," Sandy protested. "Doesn't that matter at all?"

Babs Teller just smiled. "The only thing that matters is the story," she said. "If you'd like to tell your side of it, be my guest. I'll even arrange a TV interview."

Beside Sandy both Amelia and Kenneally stirred anxiously.

"Careful," Kenneally muttered under his breath. "She's baiting you."

But his worry was unnecessary. Sandy jumped up from the deck chair. "No interview," she insisted indignantly. "You've done enough damage, and you're not going to con me into giving you more material, just so you can twist the facts around."

From behind her, Amelia offered a spirited "good girl" in encouragement.

But Babs Teller was unruffled. "Think it over, dear," she purred. "Think how much good it will do you *personally*. Just remember. There's no such thing as *bad* publicity. You should be more grateful for all this interest in you I'm creating in the public mind. When you change your mind," she added, beginning to turn away, "you'll know where to find me."

In something akin to desperation, Sandy called out, "Please leave me alone. I don't understand why you're doing this to me. Really, you don't even know me!"

There was a sly smile on Babs Teller's face when she turned around. She gave Sandy a very slow and very deliberate once-over. "Oh, *I* know *you*," she said insinuatingly, in a way that made Sandy's cheeks burn with embarrassment. "Long, long legs. Oh-so-casual, shoulder-length blond hair. Perfect skin and a body without an ounce of fat. An itsy-bitsy red bikini...No, those big blue eyes, the all-American girl-next-door looks, and especially your innocent act—you can't fool *me!* Who do you think you're talking to, sister? Some bush-league Miss Lonelyhearts? Don't ever forget, I'm Babs Teller, Hollywood's premier entertainment journalist. And you don't fool me one bit, girl. I know what, or rather *who*, you're after!" With that, she turned on her heel and in an instant was gone.

Both Kenneally and Amelia were outraged.

"Why, that vitriolic..." he began with a sputter.

"...cynical shrew," she finished in a huff.

"Don't let the witch get to you," Kenneally added. "It's an old trick. She's just trying to make you so mad you'll do or say something outrageous, something newsworthy."

"You're so right, Fitz," Amelia agreed. "You did very well not to rise to the bait, Sandy. And you can count on us to..."

Sandy's anger was boiling up. She had wanted to spit right in the hateful gossip columnist's eye, but she knew it would play right into Babs Teller's hand. Still, she was so mad she couldn't stand motionless one minute longer! She snatched up her terrycloth jacket, turned and ran heedlessly down the deck, nearly smashing into the waiter who was bringing them another round of drinks. How could she count on anybody, she thought at first, running as hard as she could. But even as she said it to herself, she knew that Amelia—and perhaps even Kenneally—was on her side.

After running a good mile around the ship's decks to keep from doing something as ridiculous as hitting the infuriating little gossip columnist or stooping to calling her a name, Sandy had blown off enough steam to say to herself, "On an ocean liner in the middle of the sea, there's nowhere to run to and certainly nowhere to hide! If she has the nerve to confront me again, she'll find out for herself why I call myself a bodyguard."

9

THE *VOYAGER QUEEN* sailed on, heading south-south-west, ever farther into the warm blue waters of the tropics.

For Sandy, each beautiful, sun-splashed day had its own particular dangers, its own treacherous currents and hidden reefs, where her reputation and her career could be wrecked on the sharp teeth of other people's ambitions. The lazy southern hemisphere days were bad, but the nights were even worse.

Each night brought another glamorous, formal evening. The sleek passengers were always elegantly dressed—the men in their tuxedos, the women wearing jewels and their finest gowns. Hundreds came together each night in the ship's Grand Ballroom, or in the Garden Lounge, or in the many other bars and hideaways all over the great ship. When all the festive, tanned pleasure-seekers were together, the dark dangers of the night could no longer be avoided.

There was Mr. Hartmann, laughing it up as always, his toothy grin showing sharp, pearly teeth.

There was the gimlet-eyed gossip columnist, slowly circling, looking for any morsels of news available, always watching Sandy to see what scandalous gaffe she would be involved in next.

There were the actors and actresses from the movie company, colorfully, attractively garbed, flitting easily in and out of the crowd.

But most of all, there was Ken Rexford, without a

doubt the most intriguing person in this glittering ocean of notables.

He socialized with the other passengers with practiced self-assurance. His aides followed along like so many pilot fish in tow. For some reason that Sandy couldn't quite fathom, Ken, after spending each day at work in isolation, made a great show of attending every possible social function at night. He seemed to enjoy mixing with the admiring crowds of his fellow passengers, exchanging small talk and banter, eating and drinking with abandon. His gregariousness and appetites knew no bounds. No subject was too big or too insignificant for him not to venture an opinion. The Ken Rexford who drifted through the swirling eddies of the nightly shipboard galas was truly the figure that Sandy recognized from the tabloids and the gossip columns.

Why did he bother to do it? Sandy wondered. She always attended, went wherever he did out of professional obligation, assuming it was her job to be nearby whenever he was out in public. Though most of the passengers were familiar to her, she never let down her guard. Her eyes constantly covered Ken's admirers and surroundings, keen to pick up anything the least bit unusual.

The formality between them then was no less painful for being obviously necessary. She always took a spot in the retinue next to Kenneally, just behind and a little to the left of Ken, from where she was poised to move forward in any eventuality. Now, of course, everyone aboard ship knew she was the Senator's bodyguard, and all the passengers were equally familiar with the on-going scandalous sensation that had been created in the press back home. But everyone acted very sophisticated, with just the right amount of politesse, joining in the transparent fiction that Fitz Kenneally was her evening escort.

Ken seemed to enjoy these social events so sinfully much that Sandy had to conclude that at least part of him had to be the playboy-bon-vivant of his reputation. It really was true, she thought to herself, standing behind him and watching him charm yet another small group before moving along to mix with others in the Grand Ballroom. But try as she might to concentrate on his bad points, Sandy was unable to forget that glade in Kauai or the way he had treated her when they were alone.

It was as if he was two different people, she said to herself in amazement, as he moved along backslapping and shaking hands and exchanging meaningless little pleasantries.

This night's festivities made Sandy especially nervous. The ship's social director had declared another "theme night." Tonight was Pirate Evening aboard the *Voyager Queen*, and everywhere there was a profusion of swords, daggers and "toy" pistols. Wherever Sandy turned she found another Jean Laffite or a Blackbeard, or an elegant noblewoman with a beehive hairdo—like a frothy cotton-candy mountain on top of her head— who was tightly corseted in a Regency gown. For the occasion, the movie company had opened its many costume trunks to the passengers, and the actors and actresses had been enlisted to play various traditional pirate roles to add to the mood and enhance the buccaneer spirit.

Both Kenneally and Harvey were dressed in colorful striped shirts and black pantaloons. "We're freebootin' rapscallions," Kenneally had announced in a credible pirate's accent, when they had all met in the hallway outside their connecting staterooms. Sandy had laughed, pleased to note just how well Fitz fitted his new role, just as she was secretly glad that Harvey looked utterly ridiculous.

Amelia looked superb, of course, in a sequined black dress. With ebony combs in her silvery hair and a shawl over her shoulders, she was every inch the grand Spanish lady. As soon as they arrived in the ballroom, she swept through the crowd to meet her dashing Captain McCabe.

Sandy was amazed at how little it took to make Ken look like a real pirate. For the most part, he was wearing his standard formal attire—the black trousers with the black satin stripe, the white ruffled shirt open at the throat and the cummerbund around his trim waist. Instead of a dinner jacket, though, he'd put on a black satin vest. From somewhere he'd gotten a matching black eye patch, which he wore rakishly tilted over one eye. A toy flint-lock pistol tucked into his waistband completed the illusion.

For once Sandy felt uncomfortable in the new gown she'd chosen to wear. Of course, the long, white-silk Empire style evening dress—with the daring bare-shoulder bodice trimmed with point d'espirit lace and with the narrow, tightly cinched waist—was absolutely perfect for the evening's theme. But it was *so* low-cut and the flimsy fingers of lace *so* emphasized her taut breasts, while barely covering them, that she couldn't help but feel too exposed, too much on display. As she moved through the gaily costumed crowd, her underskirts and petticoats rustled with every step, and she was all too aware of just where all the men's eyes were directed as she passed.

In fact, as they strolled around the edges of the dance floor, it seemed to Sandy that the only man in the entire ballroom *not* staring at her chest was Ken himself. Of course, when he'd first glimpsed her in the hallway, and everyone was admiring each other's costume, he'd gaped wide-eyed and open-mouthed at her just as all the other men were doing. He had even stepped quickly back away from her as if struck by her beauty. But since that moment he had avoided her, being as formal and circumspect as possible, as he had been ever since their return to the ship, treating her as if she were the Medusa and the sight of her might turn him instantly to stone.

As Ken's little entourage completed its second circuit of the dance floor's perimeter, the dance band switched from its jazz-flavored renditions of rousing sea chanties and began a lush, romantic ballad from the early nineteenth century. Suddenly Ken wheeled around.

"Dance?" he blurted at Sandy, sounding for all the world like a nervous teenager at the prom.

Why certainly, Sandy was about to say, reaching out for his extended hand and thinking to herself that perhaps her gown had been the appropriate choice after all, when a harsh voice croaked in her ear, "Not so fast, me lovely. First it's the turn of Cap'n Miles."

The actor was **all** decked out in the height of pirate fashion, from the tips of his pointed shoes to the top of his plumed hat. Sandy glimpsed a leather bandoleer under his purple doublet, and a cutlass hung from his waist.

To her amazement, Ken seemed genuinely angry. He put a hand around the stock of the flintlock in his cummerbund and stepped forward assertively, almost menacingly. "I believe the lady and I have this dance."

But Miles remained steadfastly in character. "No one crosses Cap'n Miles," he growled. "D'ya understand that, matey?"

Part of Sandy found it all too silly for words, but part of her—she was disconcerted to realize—found it flattering and even a little exciting to be argued over in this way. She could tell that, mixed in with the play-acting, something serious was going on.

Ken looked Miles right in the eye, giving him an icy glare. "Cap'n Miles should take care to watch his manners," he retorted in a clipped, no-nonsense tone.

Out of the corner of her eye Sandy could see Babs Teller hovering in the background. She knew she must act quickly to avoid a scene.

But just as she was about to step to Ken's side, Miles's co-star, Rose, appeared in a swirl of claret satin and ruffles. She seemed to be all raven hair and ruby lipstick and exuded an overpowering floral scent. True to her name, she had a red rose behind her ear.

Laughing gaily, she immediately latched onto Ken's elbow. "Darling, I have so wanted to meet you," she said in a fairly authentic Spanish accent. "Has anyone told you, you make an absolutely wonderful buccaneer? Don't you think so, Miles?"

The actor said nothing, but the leering grin on his face spoke volumes.

Rose continued on, unabashed. "Come, darling," she said, tugging on Ken's arm and touching the rose behind her ear, "You can dance with me. All the other ladies will be so jealous." For the first time the raven-haired actress looked at Sandy. "Won't they, dear?" she cooed.

Sandy ignored her. She glared at Ken. "Go right ahead," she said coldly. "Miles is going to dance with me."

"Good," Rose piped up, once more tugging on Ken's sleeve. "We've stood around gabbing long enough. Now, come on, Senator, let's hurry up before we miss a perfectly good number. If we do," she teased, as she led him onto the dance floor, "you'll have to dance another whole dance with me. In fact, I might make you dance more than once with me anyway."

Miles took Sandy by the arm. "That Rose, what a tiger!" he said, as they stepped onto the dance floor. "Better not get in *that* lady's way."

He slipped a hand around Sandy's waist and pulled her close to him. They began to move to the music.

Sandy whispered in Miles's ear, "Better stay out of my way, too. And don't get any ideas. I'm still furious at you, Miles."

"Hey, so I made a mistake. I was just trying to help you out. How was I to know you had your eyes on a sensational romance?" He nodded toward the other side of the floor, where Ken and Rose were dancing. "Hollywood and the Potomac," he observed. Sandy winced at his use of the phrase from the hated gossip column, but Miles didn't notice. "Your Senator is certainly a pillar of the community," he noted bitterly, "but I'm betting on our Rose. Look at that girl," he whispered, and in spite of herself Sandy glanced over at them. "What an artist, huh? She can beguile them all, great and small."

Sandy muttered ruefully, "If she was any closer to him, she'd be behind him."

Miles twirled her around in a tight little circle. "That a girl!" He laughed. "You don't take it sitting down, do you. You scratch back!"

Sandy was more than a little chagrined. She immediately saw with what pleasure Miles responded to any sign of baseness or small-mindedness in her, and she was sorry she had made the wicked remark about Rose. After all, what the actress was doing was no more than what everyone believed Sandy herself to be engaged in— namely, scheming to attract the Senator's affections.

"Miles," Sandy began thoughtfully, "I know you're going to think this sounds really naive, but why do you always think the very worst of people? I mean, it's almost as if you go out of your way to look for it."

The question brought Miles to a dead stop on the dance floor. He gave her a quizzical look. "Seriously?" he asked, pushing the plumed hat higher on his forehead.

"Uh-huh," Sandy nodded, fixing him with her blue eyes.

Miles seemed more than a little nonplussed. "I think I need a drink."

Taking her by the hand, the costumed young actor led her off the crowded dance floor and over to the well-stocked bar in a corner of the ballroom, where a red-jacketed waiter poured two long-stemmed glasses full of vintage champagne.

"Here's to the last straight-shooter in the U.S.A.," Miles said, lifting his glass in a salute. "I mean you, kid," he said in reply to her puzzled look.

"Oh, there must be many others, Miles. You just haven't met them. The world isn't as tough as you think."

"My motto, kid, is do unto others, only do it *first,* if you get my drift." He waved his glass expansively in a gesture that took in the entire ballroom. "Hell, that's what all the people here think about *you,* you know. That you're out to get yours no matter what. Am I right?"

Sandy sighed. "I know," she said glumly, sipping the sparkling champagne. "That's why everything is getting so difficult. Everybody is assuming the worst."

Everybody is assuming the worst. Her own phrase repeated itself in her brain. She was. Ken was. All those people out there were. She was assuming that Ken enjoyed being pursued by Rose. Ken was probably assuming that she was pumping Miles for details about the film world.

But what had they, Ken and she, been assuming that afternoon in the glade on Kauai? Hadn't each of them assumed strong feelings on the part of the other? Hadn't that day meant anything? On her part at least, there had been sincerity. In those hours in that tropical paradise, she had felt she loved him. But perhaps she had been seduced by her surroundings.

In any case, the solution, the *only* solution to this maze of misunderstandings, was to talk about them, point by point, without shame or embarrassment or fear of being hurt. It was the only way she and Ken would ever discover how they really felt about each other.

Nothing, she realized, could be more important. And Miles, in his own obviously selfish way, had helped her see that.

"Miles, I want you to do me a favor," she said quickly, putting the champagne glass down decisively.

"Sure, doll, anything. I guess I owe you one, huh?"

"When the music ends, Miles, I want you to go over and ask Rose to dance."

"*Me?* Dance with Rose?" Miles's lip curled with obvious distaste. "I spend twelve hours a day pretending

to be her lover for the cameras. That's enough for me,"
he said insistently. But responding to the look on Sandy's
face, he immediately relented. "Sure, doll, I'll do it for
you. I'll help you fight back. I'll just pretend it's another
scene we're doing."

Sandy didn't care what he pretended as long as he
freed Ken from Rose and gave her a chance to talk to
him. There was no time to explain anything to Miles. It
was enough that he would help. Standing on tiptoe, she
put her hands on his shoulders and gave him a peck on
the cheek. "Thank you. Thank you, Miles," she said
happily, thinking to herself that soon now all would be
well again.

With a pleased grin, he hugged her back and gave her
a big kiss in return. "It'll be a pleasure to do you a favor,"
he said.

"Being nice could get to be a habit," she told him
fondly. But he hadn't taken so much as a single step
forward when, to her horror, Sandy realized that Ken
and Rose were stopped dead in the middle of the dance
floor and were both staring at her! Even from twenty-
five feet away, Sandy could plainly see the small smile
of triumph playing across Rose's ruby lips and the look
of frozen anger on Ken's unpatched eye.

Surely he couldn't think that *meant* anything! What
conclusions was he jumping to now? That she had just
sealed an agreement for her first screen test with a kiss?
That she had kissed Miles on the dance floor in full view
of Babs Teller, hoping for additional publicity? There
was simply no telling what thoughts were going on behind the angry expression on Ken's face.

Her mind whirled. She didn't need to look around to
know that the hated gossip columnist was, in fact, nearby,
taking in the entire pantomimed scene. It didn't take any
conniving on Sandy's part to get herself into Babs's column. Already the gossip expert was probably twisting

this little incident in her warped head into innuendos and allusions that would titillate the imaginations of her millions of fans.

No matter, she thought desperately, she would go over to Ken herself and instantly explain everything.

But it was too late. Ken was still glaring directly at her, but already Rose was whispering in his ear, tugging at his sleeve.

Without once taking his eye off Sandy, Ken nodded in assent to something that Rose whispered. Still pinning Sandy to the spot where she stood with his penetrating gaze, he offered Rose his arm and the two of them left the ballroom. They seemed to glide right through the crowd of merrymakers.

"Are you okay? Hey, doll, are you okay?"

Miles's concerned voice at her ear brought Sandy out of her trance. "I'm, I'm..."

"You're pale as a ghost," he said, "and the way your nails dug into my arm..."

Instantly she released his forearm, which she had been gripping unconsciously with viselike pressure. "Sorry," she mumbled. "I, I..."

"Here, what you need is a drink," Miles said, putting a full glass of champagne into her hand.

Sandy took a large swallow of the cold, bubbling liquid, and then two more quick sips. "Sorry," she repeated, barely noticing that the third sip drained the glass. "A touch of sea sickness, I guess. Maybe I better go back up to my cabin."

"You sure?" Miles put another glass of champagne into her hand. "Listen, it's too bad I didn't get to Rose before those two left..."

"It's okay," Sandy replied tentatively, taking a small sip of the fresh champagne. "I really shouldn't be drinking anymore."

"Maybe what you need is to stay down here and party with me," Miles said, "and get that stuffed-shirt politician out of your mind. We could talk some more about your acting career."

His persistence finally broke through her reverie. "Miles, Miles, you must understand . . ." she said in exasperation, taking a last little sip of the sparkling wine before putting the glass down.

"But," Miles replied, grinning ingratiatingly, "I don't think *you* understand. Our director was taken with you as soon as he saw you. All you have to do is say the word and you've got a part in the picture. And I'm not talking bit part either."

"No Miles, it's *you,* among others, who doesn't understand that I don't *want* a part in your picture. I've got a perfectly respectable career in executive protection."

Miles pursed his lips. "Not that bodyguard stuff again."

Sandy sighed, too distraught to argue with him. She was actually woozy, too, she was beginning to realize. "I'm going up to my cabin and get some rest," she said.

"Wait, I'll come with you," Miles offered quickly, with much more enthusiasm than was required. "Wait for Cap'n Miles."

"No," Sandy said, putting a hand on his doublet to stop him. "No, I'd much rather go up myself, Miles. You just stay here and swash your buckle."

If the connecting sitting room hadn't been the only way to get to her bedroom cabin, Sandy would have been spared the sight. As it was, in the darkness she nearly missed it anyway.

The large, well-appointed sitting room was empty and no lights were on. The only illumination came from the full moon's light beaming across the silvery water and shining inside the room through the open terrace doors.

First she noticed the gossamer terrace curtains blowing gently in the tropical breeze. Then she caught sight of the silver ice bucket gleaming on top of the small wroughtiron table out on the terrace. And finally, backlighted by moonlight and the glitter of ten thousand stars . . .

She had her arms around his neck! His hands were at her waist!

Involuntarily, Sandy's hand flew to her throat, and she gasped in disbelief.

Ken jumped back from the clinging Rose. Quickly, he marched through the doors. "It's not what you think, Sandy," he told her immediately, striding toward her. "She was helping me off with my eye patch." Without looking over his shoulder, he ordered, "Tell her, Rose."

The young actress stepped gracefully through the open terrace doors. Holding the eye patch up between thumb and forefinger for Sandy to see, she confirmed with as much stagecrafted insincerity as she could muster, "Why certainly, that's *all* it was. However could you think anything else?"

Sandy backed away from them both. "I—I was just going to my room. It—it's really none of my business . . ."

"But, Sandy," Ken began. Rose smoothly cut him off.

"I don't want to intrude," she said sweetly. "I'll just be going back to my cabin."

Ken was nothing if not a gentleman, and Sandy was not surprised by his response. "I'll—I'll escort you back to your cabin," he said glumly.

"Why, how gallant," Rose said immediately, putting her arm around his elbow.

"I'll be back right away," Ken said to Sandy as he and Rose walked out of the room. "Please wait."

"Goodnight, dear," Rose added gaily over her shoulder in a tone that plainly said, *Not if I can help it, sister!*

Sandy sat primly in the center of the sitting-room couch for almost ten minutes, waiting in case Ken actually returned promptly. Then she got up and wandered disconsolately out to the terrace.

What a heartbreakingly beautiful night it was, she thought, holding on to the little terrace railing with both hands and staring out over the great ship's prow at the limpid waters and the rich velvet of the night sky, gleaming with countless exquisite stars.

How could she ever have thought it would be so simple to solve all the problems between them by talking? Ken was, after all, a public figure, a man who could someday even be President of the United States. He was single and free to escort any number of glamorous women, if he chose. If not Rose, there would always be one pretty flower or another to catch his fancy.

He was used to the jet set life. She was a monogamous creature who had lost the one person she could ever really love by the cruelest accident of fate. She and Ken Rexford were as different as night and day. Nothing, nothing could ever come of the emotions she felt for him, and the sooner she faced up to the fact, the better.

Sandy noticed that the champagne glasses next to the ice bucket on the table beside her were still untouched, so she poured herself another glass of bubbling champagne. Never again, she vowed, holding the glass up so that the moonlight was reflected in the sparkling bubbles. The calm pool of water in the idyllic Hawaiian glade flashed across her mind, but she pushed the image out. Never again, she repeated to herself. Never would she trust the kind of feelings that had engulfed her there. She would leave love to the playboys and actresses of the world. It wasn't for her.

At first tears ran silently down her cheeks, but, as the minutes passed, her eyes dried and her vision adapted to the night light. She saw that, skimming above the water far below her, was a school of flying fish, their large, translucent pectoral fins spread wing-like to catch the air currents. Sandy was amazed by the length of their flight as they raced just ahead and parallel to the ship's course. There were scores and scores of the tiny fish, like so many silvery butterflies sailing through the night. She was entranced by the magical way they would burst from the water, glide just above the tops of the waves for what seemed like hundreds of yards, dive briefly, and shoot up into the air again.

"They do that when they're being chased by predators," said a deep voice behind her.

Sandy was startled, but she didn't turn around. She didn't need to. She knew who was standing there, right behind her in the open doorway.

"It might be a shark out there," Ken continued. He paused, then said softly, "Flying is part of their mating ritual, too."

Sandy spun around then. "Mating rituals?" she repeated disbelievingly. "I might have guessed *you* would be an expert on that!"

"And you, Sandy? There are a few things you seem to be an expert on too, such as using other people to advance your own dreams."

"Which people and which dreams, Ken? Are you out of your mind?"

"Let's start with Miles. Rose tells me their director is well-connected in Hollywood and has access to all the top studios. As a 'Ten', all you'll need will be a few good introductions and you'll be on your way. And given all the press you've been getting recently—"

Sandy couldn't listen to another word of this. She had reached her boiling point. "Ken," she hissed at him, "You've put together a nice little picture, haven't you? Look, I let Mr. Hartmann think I might have some interest in becoming an actress on that first night because I didn't know if you wanted me to announce to the world that I was your bodyguard. Otherwise, the whole thing is your imagination, Ken. What do I have to do to convince you you're wrong? I've been trying to tell you that I trained in the martial arts because I'm intrigued with the field. I *like* what I do. There is a special challenge in protecting public figures, some satisfaction in foiling an assasin, for example," she said, pointedly.

"Yes," Ken said slowly. "I guess I should know better than anyone how good you are at your job. But I thought you were interested in the movie company, saw their being aboard as an opportunity—"

"Well, don't think," she cut in again. "Because you have it all wrong." She softened her voice and, stepping closer to him, held out her hand.

Where were you just now, she wanted to whisper. Why were you gone so long? But she didn't ask. They stood there quietly for a moment, the gentle sea air enveloping them, wrapping them together in the dark night.

"You see, Ken, what I've wanted to say is that Miles—"

"Miles, Rose," he interrupted, "let's not talk about them. Let's forget everything that has happened since Kauai, since that afternoon. It doesn't matter." Ken was suddenly looking at her with an intensity of desire she remembered so well.

Her heart wouldn't let her object. She wanted to go on talking, to say all the things she had been thinking, to tell him that nothing could ever work between them, that she was probably going to leave this assignment when they reached Australia.

But face to face with Ken, it somehow seemed irrelevant to try to make sense of how she felt or to try to unravel the mysteries in which she was entwined. Back in the ballroom, talking everything out had seemed the answer, but now that her skin was touching his, words seemed unimportant. Only one language mattered now, and it was the language that knew no misunderstandings, no embarrassment—the language of touch. In the darkness, his eyes fastened on her with laserbeam intensity. All the light of the stars and the full moon seemed to be reflected in those eyes. They pinned her to the spot like twin beams freezing prey. If a tidal wave had come out of nowhere to sweep them both overboard, it wouldn't have mattered. Nothing mattered but the moment and the magnetism. Once again, everything else fell away, and there was only Sandy and the man and their timeless dance of love.

"Sandy," he whispered, "I'm sorry if I misunderstood." He pulled her close to him. "Sandy," he repeated, so softly that it might have been the night breeze calling her name. "Tonight nothing matters but you and me," he told her, taking her into his arms.

Yes, yes, she thought, realizing how utterly fitting those few simple words were.

He kissed her bare shoulder and the nape of her neck. He raised his head, slowly, slowly, brushing his lips lightly up her neck, all the way to the very tip of her up-stretched chin. His lips hovered over hers.

"Yes," she whispered back to him, as a rapture of delight cascaded through her expectant body. "Nothing matters . . ."

His forceful kiss was almost unbearable ecstasy. His probing tongue explored her willing mouth.

One hand held her, pressing firmly against the small of her back. His other hand stroked the soft skin of her cheek, her neck, her gracefully rounded shoulder and down her smooth, bare arm. The thrill of fiery pleasure followed his touch.

Gently, he cupped her breast in his hand . . .

From somewhere far away came the faintest of noises, then . . .

The door of the sitting room flew open. There was a flash of light, as blinding as it was brief.

The door slammed shut as suddenly as it had opened, and Sandy heard the muffled sound of feet running rapidly down the hallway.

Someone had just taken their picture!

*   *   *

Amelia, Kenneally, and Harvey were all still in costume when they burst through the sitting-room door only a few moments later. But they didn't look as if they were in a party mood. Sandy could tell from the worried looks on their faces that something was wrong. But it wasn't quite what she thought.

Amelia spoke first. "The Captain and I were out walking on deck," she said. "It was such a lovely night and there was so much noise in the ballroom. When we passed the wireless office, Babs Teller was just coming out. What a horrid person! She had such a gloating look on her face that, as soon as she was gone, I convinced dear Captain McCabe to go in and find out what she was up to. And it was lucky I did.

"Sparky—he's the man who sends out the messages—said she had just run in demanding to send another story back to the States instantly and that she was terribly excited and insistent that it go out that very second. Sparky complied, of course. What else could he do?"

Kenneally reached inside his striped sailor's shirt and pulled out a smudged piece of paper. "Here's the damn carbon," he growled, handing it to Ken.

Although Ken had been assuring Sandy that he didn't blame her for the picture-taking, and that together they would deal with the problem, he had not seemed so upset about it as Sandy herself was. Now, as he scanned the paper, his handsome face widened into an amused grin. Aloud, he read excerpts from the gossip columnist's wireless transmission:

> "'...hot news from the love cruise, dear readers...new romantic twists in that Hollywood-Washington love triangle I clued you in on in my last dispatch...that torrid twosome that was in danger of turning into a tingling threesome is now a fascinating foursome...yes, dear readers, I just

*heard it straight from one of the participants her-
self...I can't reveal who she is, but let's just say
that our Senator's latest plaything is a gorgeous
young actress who was blushing ROSE red when
she confided in your humble correspondent...'*

"I've read enough." Ken chuckled gently, offering the
carbon copy to Sandy. "It seems you're now *'the spurned
blonde bombshell.'*"

Sandy winced and turned away. She stepped over to
the couch and sat down wordlessly, too sickened by the
whirl of rumor and gossip, and the prospect of more
distress to come, to speak a single word.

She was also dumbfounded at Ken's reaction to this
vicious gossip, by now probably being read from coast
to coast in the United States. He had been distressed
enough at the first dispatch, had stormed off with his
aides to puzzle out who could have betrayed Ken's private life so cruelly. But now he stood there amused at
the whole thing. The thought of their photograph shooting over the wires and into thousands of newspapers...even that hadn't seemed to alarm him.

How could she have believed even for one foolish
second that she could find happiness with Ken Rexford?
He *wanted* to be seen as the playboy he was. How de-
luded she had been only a few minutes ago by the strength
of his embrace, by the electricity of his touch. Her chances
of being happy with him were about as good, she concluded, as one of those flying fish out there gliding up
to the moon! And she would never understand him.

But the turn the conversation was taking, and what
Amelia was saying, snapped her out of her reverie.

"At least this time, dear brother," she was telling Ken
pointedly, "you *must* know that Sandy is not responsi-
ble."

Sandy was surprised when curmudgeonly old Kenneally came to her defense as well. "It wasn't the last

time either, was it Harvey?" He turned to the junior aide.
"Come on, Harvey, tell him. Confession is good for the
soul."

"I had nothing to do with what happened tonight,"
Harvey sputtered. "I've hardly spoken to that gossip columnist at all."

"Slick, Harvey," Kenneally retorted. "But we're not
talking about tonight—at least not yet. We're talking
about how all this got started. We're talking about who
blabbed from Kauai."

Harvey's face twisted up and got very red. He stut-
tered, mumbled something incomprehensible, started to
speak and stopped. He was standing next to Ken and the
two seemed to exchange an almost conspiratorial glance,
but still he said nothing.

Kenneally's expression was even more sour than usual.
"I guess you have to have a soul before confession is of
any use, right lad?" he asked sarcastically.

Ken held up a restraining hand as Harvey looked toward him in an obvious appeal for help. "I know that
Harvey is the one who reported the incident on Kauai to
the press. He has told me all about it," he said in a
dignified voice. It was as though he wasn't talking about
an intimate moment in his own life at all, Sandy thought.

Amelia let out a gasp. "Harvey had his reasons, and
I think it's best if we all drop the subject . . . for now,"
Ken continued. "However, Sandy is the one who has
been most hurt by all the gossip, and I do think Harvey
owes her an apology."

Harvey seemed to spring at the opportunity like a
drowning man going after a life preserver. Instantly, he
rushed over to where Sandy was and, much to her surprise, put an arm around her shoulder. "I had nothing to
do with this one, I swear it, Sandy," he said fervently.
"Please believe me. If I had known how much it would
hurt you, I never would have come up with the scheme
I did. I thought it would help Senator Rexford . . . I

mean . . . I had a plan . . . and I thought you could use the publicity . . . I didn't realize . . ."

"Publicity!" Sandy exploded. "Do you think the Executive Protection Agency wants a *blonde bombshell* on its staff? What will happen to my career after all this?"

Ken stepped over to Harvey and Sandy. "Don't worry about your career, Sandy. When this trip is over, I'm sure I can offer an explanation of everything to your agency. It really won't be a problem."

A word from Ken to the right people, and all the rumors would be erased? Sandy thought. He hadn't freed himself of his own spicey reputation, she noticed. She looked toward Amelia for advice.

"As cruel as it all seems, dear, I think we'll have to trust Ken in this. He has sight of the larger issues," Amelia said.

Sandy nodded. Amelia had good judgment and whatever Harvey had done and whatever his reasons, Sandy felt it was only good manners to accept his apologies. He seemed so sincere and, seeing him standing there in his costume, she had to smile.

"I suppose anyone can make a mistake, Harvey," she said. He took her hand and kissed it in complete seriousness.

"Thank you, Sandy," he said. "Thank you."

"We do have another little problem," Ken announced. Knowing what he was about to say, Sandy couldn't understand the lightness of his tone. His changed attitude was more than she could fathom.

Delicately, but as if it was all in a day's fun, he proceeded to explain to his sister and his two aides about the clandestine picture. "I was looking at something in Sandy's eye just at the exact moment the flash went off. Unfortunately, it could easily be misinterpreted in the photograph . . ."

"Yes, how 'unfortunate,'" Kenneally agreed dryly,

and Sandy knew he wasn't taken in for a moment.

Ken ignored his trusted aide's not-so-subtle dig and turned to Sandy, his tone becoming more serious. "I think I understand about this latest gossip column," he said. "You see, when I took Rose back down to her cabin, she threatened blackmail unless I—shall we say— 'showed her more attention.' She said she'd go right to Babs Teller. From the sound of it, that's exactly what she did do."

Oddly, Sandy's reaction to this news was one of relief. She was pleased to hear that Ken's lengthy absence had this sort of explanation. Gradually, Sandy was coming to more than one realization.

"I've been thinking about the picture, trying to re-construct the moment in my mind," she told Ken. "Just before the door was thrown open, I heard a sound—a very faint sound, but enough to make me more alert to the direction it was coming from. I looked out of the corner of my eye just a fraction of a second before the blinding light. It was very dark, and I'm not at all certain, but that may have been Mr. Hartmann crouched in the doorway, taking our picture."

"Good girl," Amelia chimed in immediately. "That's doing your job." To her brother she added, "I saw Hartmann and that shrew of a gossip columnist talking together just after you all left the party. By the time the Captain and I went out on deck for our walk, neither of them was to be seen."

Kenneally nodded thoughtfully. "Shall we get our lawyers in on this? If they hear from our people, that should make them think twice before they try anything more."

"No," Ken replied. "It'll just add fuel to the fire. Besides, we've only got circumstantial evidence that Hartmann and Babs Teller are colluding in this."

Sandy shook her head, wondering at his seeming lack

of concern. Maybe hers was the only reputation pure enough to *be* tarnished by all of this. We've only got circumstantial evidence, she thought to herself, but...they've got the picture!

10

IN THE BRILLIANT light of another perfect South Pacific day, things looked much better, Sandy decided. Standing on the fantail and breathing the fresh sea air helped her feel that her prospects were much improved.

For one thing, Harvey's admission had removed the cloud of suspicion that she had felt herself under for the last several days. It didn't explain why he had clued in the press on Kauai, but Sandy had decided to trust Ken's promise that he'd eventually explain.

For another thing, there was a string of beautiful islands to explore.

While she had slept, the *Voyager Queen* had slipped into the harbor at Suva, on the island of Viti Levu, the picturesque little capital of the independent Nation of Fiji, a necklace of some 300 tropical volcanic islands and coral reefs spread over more than 7,000 square miles of the Pacific. Once a colony of Britain, the Fijis retained a good deal of the charm and atmosphere of a nineteenth century British colonial outpost, combined with the exotic, timeless way of life of Melanesia.

Sandy had on pale lavender, pleated silk shorts and a light-brown, short-sleeve cotton sweater with a scoop neck. Over the shorts, she wore a matching wraparound skirt, belted at the waist and unbuttoned in the front, so that the skirt fluttered free in the hibiscus-scented breeze. Beside her was her overnight bag, packed for the next phase of her journey.

Once again island-hopping was the order of the day. Amelia had been scheduled to explore one of the smaller nearby islands to study a site for a potential tourist hotel, but she had again begged off. This time the cause was not sea sickness, but love sickness. She had confided to Sandy and Ken early that morning that she found it impossible to turn down Captain McCabe's offer to accompany him for a day of sight-seeing on Suva, and that she was fully aware that the Captain couldn't stray far from his ship. She had begged her brother to take over for her.

Ken was scheduled to give a speech at South Pacific University in Suva, where he would also have a few private meetings with unnamed dignitaries. Still, he did not feel free to tell Sandy whom he would see, and why. But he had briefed her on what his moves would be, where he wanted her, and which buildings would have to be under top security.

"I don't expect any gunmen this time." He had smiled. "But you never know. These talks are sensitive, and a lot of people could be interested in seeing that they don't succeed."

Sandy was feeling less irritated by all the mystery. Watching the seriousness on Ken's face whenever he mentioned the work he was doing behind his closed door, she could sense its importance. It made her feel her job had been necessary after all. She hadn't been sure in the beginning that the vacationing Senator would need her skills. Now she not only felt needed, she even felt somewhat appreciated.

After the morning at the University, Ken was scheduled to make a visit to the interior by seaplane, to the part of the island where his family owned property. In addition, the natives living near the site had planned entertainment for him in their village.

Evidently Ken's aides were not to be included in this part of the trip, but Sandy, as bodyguard, was. Again

she was being put in the position of being away with
Ken overnight, alone.

Standing now on the fantail of the *Voyager Queen*,
watching the Hartmanns joining a boatload of passengers
going ashore, Sandy was only too conscious of how it
would seem when it became known—and surely it must,
one way or another—that the Senator and his bodyguard
had gone away for the night. But when she had broached
the certainty of more gossip to Ken, he had seemed
supremely unconcerned.

"Let them talk," he'd said airily, pausing over his
breakfast of grapefruit and coffee, which had been served
to him on the terrace of his stateroom. "After all, we'll
have the entire population of a native village as chap-
erones. Tell them that."

Even Kenneally had seemed relatively sanguine about
the prospect of their side trip fanning the flames of scandal. "Let 'em whisper," he'd rasped, when she voiced
her concerns to him. "We'll be havin' the last word yet."

What could she do? Being with Ken was the essential
part of her assignment. Now, as he stood next to her in
a white linen suit and blue-and-white striped shirt, he
seemed totally relaxed. They stepped into the small motor
launch that would take them across Suva harbor, and
already her sharp eyes were "on duty," scouring their
surroundings for possible dangers. Her worries over her
reputation left her.

When they reached the buildings of the university,
Ken was met by a brigade of men. As in Hawaii, his
colleagues seemed to be dressed in the costumes of several nations, and again a few burnooses from Mauristan
were evident. Sandy could hardly sort them out before
Ken was swept into a conference room. She posted herself outside the door.

His meetings were fairly brief—groups of delegates
coming and going a few times in the course of the morning, always escorted by local police. Then Ken was led

to the auditorium to speak. Sandy followed close behind
him, aware of the pressure of her holster on her upper
chest as she walked along, alert to every sound and motion.

It was a minor speech . . . public relations for his family really. It seemed strange somehow that Ken had asked
his hosts to bar all press coverage of his talk and meetings, which he had told her earlier he had done. In the
first few sentences, Sandy learned that his family had
owned a nearby island for more than one hundred years.
Ken knew a great deal about its history and traditions
and referred to local events and customs throughout his
talk.

The main point of his appearance here was clothed in
the final paragraphs of his speech. He concluded by giving much reassurance to those assembled that any plans
his family had to develop the island would be strictly
limited to the far side and to a single, tastefully designed
resort hotel that would be approved of by the building
commissioner of the island.

The applause was enthusiastic when he finished, and
Ken beamed his best professional smile out over the
assortment of cotton-clad natives, business-suited gentlemen, and students as he came out of the auditorium.

Just as he stepped out of the building, Sandy caught
the fast, nervous motion of a dark-haired boy wearing
khakis. He was pushing his way through the wall of
people closest to Ken and now stood facing him only
inches away.

Sandy was next to Ken in a moment, placing her body
between him and his assailant, her hands frisking expertly
the boy's tan army shirt and slacks. He was not armed.
He was only angry.

"You'll never get away with it, Senator Rexford," he
bellowed in a loud, deep voice. "You think you can solve
everybody's problems, just because your family owns

half the world's oil. But others have a right to it too, you know! You..."

Three or four native policemen with guns strapped to their waists were quickly on either side of the boy, dragging him off to a waiting police jeep at the curb.

Sandy didn't leave Ken's side even when he stepped into a waiting bullet-proof limousine. The police had told her it was impenetrable. She slipped into the car beside him and rolled up the window near her, her hand poised instinctively on her shoulder holster.

"Never a dull moment, is there, Sandy?" Her own heart was beating wildly, and she was amazed at Ken's cool, unruffled appearance. "I'm somewhat used to this, you know, and he was only a harmless, local student. Students have opinions on everything. But thank you for your expert protection."

Suddenly Sandy knew why her stomach was churning, why her palms were wet. She wasn't usually this upset when she was called on to step between a client and an assailant. But she couldn't keep the picture of Ken being hurt, Ken being wounded, Ken being killed, out of her mind. The crack of an assassin's gun echoed in her ears as if it were real, as real as the crack of Philly's gun, which had sounded again and again in her head during these past long months...

This hadn't been a close call. It was only an anti-capitalist student, or some such. Nevertheless, Sandy was swallowing back tears that seemed to be collecting in a hard knot in her throat. She was relieved when they reached Suva harbor again, and she was forced to concentrate on the next event of the day. Arrangements had been made for Ken and Sandy to board a seaplane that would take them off to the native village. Soon they were airborne. As they took off, the pilot—a grizzled island rat—remarked, "Next stop, folks, the matchless, bee-óotiful Blue Lagoon."

* * *

As soon as she saw it, Sandy knew exactly what the pilot had meant. A wide blue lagoon was fringed by a score of palm-covered islands.

"Did you mean the Blue Lagoon, from the movie?" Sandy asked, shouting to make herself heard above the loud buzz of the engine.

"Yes, ma'am," the pilot, a weather-beaten native of the islands, said. "I don't know exactly which one of them little gems down there they filmed it on, but I guess it don't really matter none. I mean, you can tell from up here, one's more beautiful than the next—white beaches, green forest, blue water. Every single one of these little islands in Bligh's Sea is like that."

"Bligh's Sea?" Sandy repeated.

"Yes, ma'am," the pilot said, concentrating on slowly banking the seaplane as he prepared to land in the peaceful lagoon. "That's what folks call the waters in this part of the archipelago. Been known as Bligh's Waters ever since Captain Bligh was thrown off the *Bounty* and came through here in an open longboat, heading for the Dutch East Indies. At one time all the Fijis was called Bligh's Islands."

"You're talking about *Captain* Bligh?" Sandy questioned. "The one in 'Mutiny on the Bounty'?"

"Yes, ma'am," the pilot said once again, throttling back the engine and bringing the seaplane skimming along the water's calm surface. "I hear they made a movie outa that story, too," he added, cutting off the engine. The little seaplane bobbed on the peaceful blue water.

Behind Sandy, Ken was packing up his briefing books. "Are you beginning to see why the family's considering building a hotel here?" he asked dryly. "How does *Bligh's Blue Lagoon Resort* sound?"

Sandy laughed appreciatively, and Ken turned to the pilot. "Going back or staying the night, Duff?"

"Staying the night, Senator," the pilot replied.

"How're we going to get to shore?" Sandy asked curiously, looking around the seaplane's small cabin for a raft.

"We could swim," Ken said. He pointed out the plane's window. "Or we could take a Fiji taxi."

Looking out too, Sandy was surprised to see a long outrigger canoe coming toward them. Four bare-chested, dark-skinned, smiling men were paddling it.

"This *is* like 'Mutiny on the Bounty'," she said in amazement.

"The real thing." Ken chuckled and returned the Fijians' waves of greeting.

Once ashore, Sandy saw the small village of thatched huts nestled among the palm and mangrove trees just beyond the shoreline. There they were welcomed with a great deal of ceremony by the villagers, who were wearing *tapa* skirts colorfully decorated with geometric patterns. After drinking bowls of strong *yaqona*, their bags were taken to a large *bura*, or thatched hut. The village elder, speaking in a deep, very British accent, formally extended to the Senator and his companion free run of the entire island.

"Let's go exploring," Ken said happily, abruptly taking Sandy by the hand and starting off into the jungle as he waved goodbye to the villagers.

"What royal treatment," Sandy said as they walked. "You really are the big chief here." She fingered the necklace of exquisite white coral that a native girl had slipped around her neck.

"Well, my family has gotten along well with the natives since late in the last century."

"And you're going to build a hotel here?" Sandy asked dubiously. All around them the jungle displayed its profusion of natural splendor—coconut palms; mangroves; breadfruit, tamarind and casuarina trees; frangipangi, pointsettia and hibiscus—a hundred varieties of plants growing in colorful abundance. "I mean, you really won't ruin all this—the forest, the villagers' way of life?"

"So far, wherever we've put up hotels we've managed to preserve local life pretty well. And if we don't develop these places, somebody else will. Besides, the natives are all for it. And if *we* build it, the hotel's going to be on the other side of the island, well away from the village."

"I don't know," Sandy said. She squeezed Ken's hand. "It's so beautiful here. I'd hate to see it change."

"Don't worry," Ken said as they made their way along a path between rows of tall mangroves, "I wouldn't allow anyone to do anything here to damage this way of life. I promise, nobody's going to bulldoze those thatched huts or uproot the bougainvillea."

His mention of thatched huts reminded Sandy of something she'd noticed before. "Ken," she said quietly, "the villagers put both of our bags into the same hut. They don't expect us to stay overnight in the same one, do they? That's not exactly chaperoning..."

Ken laughed. "Does that worry you?" he asked, pulling her closer to him and putting his arm around her shoulder.

Sandy pulled away again, frowning. "Not for the reason you think," she told him. "It's just that I'd hate to give any more ammunition to the gossips back on the ship."

"But who's going to know *what* we do here?"

Sandy shrugged. "Who would have thought we'd be spied on from a helicopter in Kauai," she replied with a sigh. "I mean, the pilot seems nice enough and all the villagers are so friendly, but after what we've been through, who knows?"

"Anyway," she added firmly, "we still have a lot to settle between us, don't we? I mean, we're getting along so well now, but..."

"But you don't trust me, is that it?" he finished for

her. "Sandy, I will explain a great deal to you, as soon as I can. I've told you that."

Sandy sighed deeply, but said nothing.

Ken thought for a moment. "Oh," he said, "if it's how I acted that night when I saw you and Miles in the stateroom, I realize I was wrong. It's easy to jump to conclusions when you've had as many bad experiences with women as I have. Just look at what happened with Rose and how she tried to blackmail me with Babs Teller. My only excuse is that I was jealous when I saw you and Miles together."

Sandy was glad to hear this confession, but it didn't put her completely at ease. "It's okay," she said in a whisper. "I *can* see why you jumped to that kind of conclusion about Miles and me. I *do* appreciate just how much a man in your position has to worry about conniving women out to use him. I mean, your looks, your fame, your fortune—you're the perfect target for a golddigger."

Ken was obviously pleased. "Thank you," he said happily, "I'm not used to this kind of understanding... not from a beautiful woman *or* a straight-arrow cop," he added with a smile, "and certainly not from *both* rolled up in one person." He stopped suddenly. "Hey, you know the only cloud within a thousand miles is the one crossing your beautiful face. What's bothering you?"

Sandy took a deep breath of fragrant air. "It's silly, I know, but even here on this beautiful island I can't forget who you are and that I'm just a bodyguard. And... and sometimes, I don't know, you seem so different. I can't really explain it."

Ken let go of her hand. "Then how can I deal with it? I'll do, say anything you want. Just tell me what will reassure you about me."

"I... I don't know yet," Sandy admitted.

They walked on through the jungle paradise in silence.

Sandy tried to focus in on what was bothering her, to remember where it had all begun. So much had happened in such a short time. It was hard to sort it all out in her mind.

Was it simply being courted by a man who could someday be a candidate for the highest office in the United States? Was it something in herself? Was she frightened to fall in love with him so precipitously when she had been so sure she would never love again?

Or was it something in *him?* It upset Sandy that he seemed so casual and unconcerned in the face of the scandal beginning to rage around them both, and also that he seemed to relish the trivial, backslapping sociability of the professional politician.

She remembered all the way back to when she had first seen him—the sardonic look, the way he'd grabbed her and kissed her before they had even exchanged a word in that broom closet in the Capitol Building. *That* was it, she realized. Ken had never explained *that,* and it had colored everything that had come after. She turned to him with a questioning look on her face.

"Look!" he cried. "Look at that beach! Did you ever see anything like that in your life?" Already he was running ahead, dashing between two palm trees and out onto the white sand. "Come on," he called out, turning and waving as he ran. "Let's forget our troubles! It's too beautiful! Let's go for a swim!"

Sandy had to smile in spite of herself—both at his boyish exuberance and at the utterly lovely stretch of gently curving, white sand beach ahead. The deserted little beach, framed by swaying palms, the sparkling blue cove. Surely this was the setting for every tropical-paradise movie ever made, she thought, beginning to run toward the pristine sand.

By the time she caught up with him, his shirt and his shoes were already off, and he was beginning to unfasten the top button of his white shorts.

She came to an abrupt stop next to him, just above the tide line, and kicked off her shoes. "Wait a minute, Ken," she said with a big smile. "In all this excitement, I forgot one little detail. I didn't bring a bathing suit."

When had she seen such a big, engagingly boyish grin outside of a playground? Sandy wondered.

"No problem," Ken said. "I didn't bring one either." And before she could say or do anything other than gasp, he'd unzipped the shorts, let them fall around his ankles and, in one neat motion, kicked them into the air. She was still standing there when he turned and dashed, naked, into the surf and dove into the inviting blue waters.

A second later his head bobbed up several yards from shore, and he waved at her. "Come on in," he called out. "The water's just fine."

"Are you crazy?" she shouted back. "What if someone's looking? Or what if there's somebody with a camera behind a palm tree?"

"Then I hope they snapped my good side," he yelled back, sounding utterly unconcerned. "Come on in."

Sandy shook her head. "You've gone crazy!"

"No, not crazy," he said in a booming voice, beginning to float on his back. "Just gone native."

"I'm not taking off my clothes and coming in there, not on your life," Sandy vowed. "That kind of trouble I do not need!"

He began to do a lazy back stroke. "Could be a fierce, man-eating shark under water," he teased. "Or maybe a giant octopus like in *Twenty Thousand Leagues Under the Sea*. You can't protect my body from way out there, now can you, Ms. Bodyguard?"

"Okay, *Senator,*" she said, giving in to her urges, "you win."

She untied her wraparound skirt and let it fall to the sand. Then, as unselfconsciously as possible, she pulled the brown sweater up over her head and threw it on top of the skirt. She was only too aware that she wasn't wearing a bra.

When Ken, still floating several yards from shore, called out "Bravo!" she stuck her tongue out at him. She unbuttoned the pleated shorts, hooked her thumbs under the waistband, and stepped out of them. For a second she considered whether or not to keep on her white-silk bikini panties. Then she decided not to be coy. It didn't matter anyway, she told herself, because the panties were totally transparent when wet.

"Magnificent!" Ken shouted out when she was completely unclothed. As she ran into the water, he let out a joyful, exulting whoop.

The only sound was the hiss of air bubbles as she dived below the surface of the calm blue water. When she opened her eyes, she was in a bright, colorful wonderland. Rainbow-hued tropical fish darted through crystal-clear water. Fantastic coral shapes grew up from the ocean floor lined with shellfish. Two delicate little fish, like butterflies of the sea, darted past her head. Below her swam a turtle, describing slow, graceful S-curves between the projecting coral outcroppings. She propelled herself slowly through this silent kingdom of otherworldly beauty.

She looked up. Ken was just a dark form on the surface. Then he turned, curled, extended and shot past her in a long, graceful dive. Slowly he circled until he was swimming alongside her.

She couldn't help but notice the rhythmic motion of the strong muscles in his flanks and shoulders as he stroked through the water. How trim his waist was, and how broad and powerful his chest. It was a swimmer's body, she thought, remembering an impossibly long-ago and far-away winter's day when she'd sat in her cold Washington apartment re-reading his file. *Captain, Harvard Swim Team* the entry had read. She could tell from the way he looked and how he moved through the water that he hadn't lost his form or his power.

She tapped him on the shoulder, pointed to the surface, and began immediately to ascend to the world of sunlight and oxygen. He nodded, joining her for the glide to the surface. As they floated lazily toward the light, he put his arm around her waist, and she felt a thrill of almost electric intensity radiate through her body from the sensuousness of his touch.

They broke the surface together, laughing and gasping for breath. Water was still streaming down her face when he kissed her.

One moment she was treading water next to him and the next she was in his arms, her eyes closed, falling backwards in languorous slow motion through the sparkling blue depths.

The kiss and the embrace lasted until the need for air sent them racing back up to the surface again. She was still trying to catch her breath when he reached out to pull her close to him again.

"Ken, please, no." She put a hand up to hold him back.

"Something the matter?" he asked, playfully splashing water at her.

She splashed back, but her heart wasn't in it. "I do so want to . . . be here with you. Believe me, there's nothing I want more. It's just that I can't get out of my mind what we were talking about before."

He looked at her thoughtfully through water-drop-laden lashes. To her relief, he was taking what she was saying seriously.

"I'm not toying with you. This isn't a game with me," he pronounced, gulping water. "You're so beautiful, Sandy," he whispered, moving toward her.

This time she let him take her in his arms again. She let him press his body against hers. She met his passion with her own, opening her mouth to receive his probing tongue, wrapping her hands around his neck, her legs around his waist.

Again they sank beneath the calm blue waters of the lagoon, descending slowly in a cloud of trembling bubbles, enveloped in a rapture of delight.

They rose again, letting the gentle waves carry them together to the edge of the water, where they made love, sinuously entwining their two wet bodies. They touched, they caressed, they moved together in rhythm with the sea. And after a small eternity, after their passion was finally spent, only then did they seem to rejoin the world of air and sky.

They pulled themselves farther up on the shore and collasped in each other's arms, lying where they fell— where the sea met the sand—and letting the warm sun dry their wet, naked bodies.

By the time they returned to the little village, the sun was only a faint orange glow on the darkening western horizon and a large, open fire was blazing on the village commons. A festival was in progress!

After being welcomed back by the village *Ratu*, or chief, and sipping from the ceremonial bowl of *yaqona*, the strong, throat-numbing native drink, Sandy and Ken took the place of honor in the long line of swaying dancers. Sandy wondered fleetingly what had happened to Duff, their pilot.

It was a timeless, totally authentic scene, with none of the compromises usually made for tourists' tender sensibilities. Here there were no guitars or ukuleles, no porkpie hats. The villagers wore feathers and shells and plaited *tapa* skirts. The women danced bare-breasted. The musicians, their faces masked and painted, pounded drums, beat bamboo sticks, and shook hollow gourds to the throbbing, insistent beat.

As the villagers chanted and snake-danced around the leaping fire, the musicians beat out a rhythmic tattoo of ever-increasing frenzy. These were the real island dances, Ken told Sandy as they joined the general revelry, whose origins went back to ancient fertility rites and dark practices from the time when the Fijis were known and feared as the Cannibal Isles.

Sandy had felt exhausted before, trudging back to the village, but the strong beat of the festive dances and the powerful draughts of *yaqona* that she drank to quench her thirst revived her flagging energies. Soon she and Ken were snake-dancing and doing the hip-bumping *tar-alala* dance with complete abandon.

The long, golden evening passed in another kind of ecstasy. Afterwards, when Ken and Sandy indicated to their hosts and hostesses that they were tired, a small group of them took torches and gestured that they should follow. To the beat of drums, Ken and Sandy were led to their thatched *bura*, the one in which their bags had been left. It was clear that the natives intended them to sleep together in the hut. Either they thought she and Ken were married, or they didn't value such formalities.

This was no time to argue, and Sandy, bone-weary, let herself be led, her hand in Ken's, to the bamboo mat inside. There they made slow, dreamily tender love.

While she lay naked on the mat, Ken spread the coconut-scented oil that the villagers used on ceremonial occasions all over her body. He massaged her slowly, sensuously, from the tops of her shoulders to the tips of her toes.

When he was finished at last, she whispered throatily, "I'll do you, too."

But he just shushed her. She could barely hear his husky voice as he bent over and kissed her belly. "First I'll lick it off."

He seemed to be savoring her, as if she was some indescribably delicious tropical delight, and the light touch of his mouth against her skin sent her into renewed paroxysms of utterly exquisite frenzy. She arched wildly to the flick of his tongue, feeling an incredible longing to give him as much pleasure as he was giving her. And so it wasn't until the open fire outside had burned down to crackling, glowing embers, and the first, faint light of the rose-fingered dawn touched the distant horizon, that they finally fell asleep in each other's arms.

11

THEY DIDN'T LEAVE the small island until mid-morning, not until after a delicious tropical breakfast of *cassava*, coconut milk, bananas, and pineapple.

The grizzled pilot seemed more than a little out of sorts as he guided the seaplane across the blue lagoon and up into the azure sky for the short flight back to the port city of Suva, where the *Voyager Queen* was waiting.

Sandy felt wonderful. She sat in the copilot's chair, her left arm draped casually over the back of the seat, holding Ken's hand. Turning to the pilot and favoring him with a big, sunny smile, she said, "We didn't see you at the festival last night, Mr. Duff. Didn't you feel well?"

"Not with all them half-dressed pagans running around I didn't," he replied irritably. "I kept inside my thatched hootch all night with a good book and a bottle. I wanted no part of that heathen ceremony."

Sandy was surprised by this harshly condemning attitude from a man who lived his life among the gentle island people, but Ken's warning pressure on her hand alerted her not to say anything more.

The pilot glanced at her out of the corner of his eye. "Say," he asked slyly, "I didn't know you had been married, Senator."

Though the comment wasn't directed at her, Sandy felt compelled to answer. "I, that is, we..."

Behind her, Ken interjected smoothly. "We *plan* to be, Duff."

"Oh, is that so?" Duff replied. Again he gave Sandy an appraising glance. "Well, you're a mighty lucky man, Senator, a mighty lucky man indeed."

"Thank you, Duff," Ken said.

Sandy twisted around in her chair and gave Ken a tentative smile and a questioning look. Ken smiled back and blew her a silent kiss, and Sandy wondered how he could tell a lie with such conviction.

But there wasn't much time to think about that or the implications of the pilot's remark. The short airplane ride back to Suva passed in silence, and the day was much too beautiful for Sandy to dwell on such a small cloud. She held Ken's hand and watched the lovely ocean view out of the plane's window until the mountains and the twin bays of Fiji's bustling capital city appeared ahead.

It wasn't long before the surly pilot was just a faint memory, and she and Ken were strolling hand in hand through the quaint, colonial streets of the town's markets, passing the time until the ship's scheduled sunset departure.

Up ahead was a charmingly rustic East Indian restaurant with an outdoor patio and a good view of the many duty-free shops lining the narrow street. Seated at a big, prominent table was a tour party from the *Voyager Queen*. Sandy was mildly surprised to see both Amelia and Kenneally there, but she was even more surprised that Mr. and Mrs. Hartmann were seated with them. On the table was a pot of steaming tea and a large revolving wooden tray containing a sampler of native foods.

As soon as she spotted them, Amelia immediately waved them over. Sandy was about to extricate her hand from Ken's grasp, but he just tightened his grip.

"Not on your life," he whispered. *"Let* the world know." He beamed.

Amelia took charge of pouring them tea as soon as they sat down. "Ceylonese Silver Tip," she said. "I was just talking about the tea with the proprietor, an Indian chap from Bombay. It's the finest buds from the best of the crop, you know, with a lovely bouquet and delightful astringent taste. And it seems that he gets his supply from our plantation in Sri Lanka. Isn't that a coincidence, Ken?"

"Quite a small world," Ken agreed, taking a sip of the tea and eyeing Mr. Hartmann, who had been openly sneering at Ken and Sandy from the moment they had sat down.

"Isn't it," Amelia agreed. "The proprietor was kind enough to offer us this delightful brunch, so Fitz and I invited Mr. and Mrs. Hartmann over to share it."

"Yes, and I think we should get back to our table," Mr. Hartmann said without a trace of sociability, much less friendliness.

"Oh, don't go," Amelia said quickly. "We were having such an interesting conversation."

"Yeah, Senator," Kenneally interjected pointedly, "we were just beginning to discuss our mutual interest in photography, weren't we, Mr. Hartmann?"

"I don't think we have any more to talk about," Mr. Hartmann snarled, beginning to stand. "Come, dear."

Mrs. Hartmann, who had been busily eating, looked up, nodded, and dabbed at her lips with a napkin. "Delicious," she said. "Thank you."

Amelia's courteous smile didn't falter once. "Here," she said, offering one of the dishes on the revolving tray to Mrs. Hartmann. "We have so much and you're enjoying the *kokoda*. Do take it with you."

"No, no, I couldn't," Mrs. Hartmann protested, but when Amelia insisted that the Fijian delicacy—raw fish marinated in lime juice and coconut cream—was not to be passed up, she took the bowl and followed her husband to their table a few yards away.

"That woman," Amelia observed in amazement to Sandy. "You'd think she hadn't eaten in a week. She devoured an entire bowl of bêche-de-mer!"

"Bêche-de-mer?" Sandy repeated questioningly, aware that Kenneally, seated across the table, was telling Ken in an undertone that they had made no progress with the Hartmanns.

Amelia made a little grimace of distaste. "Sea slugs," she whispered. "If Mrs. Hartmann knew what she was eating, I bet she'd gag."

Kenneally and Ken got up in tandem. "Would you excuse us for a few minutes?" Ken said. "Fitz and I are going for a little stroll so he can brief me on developments."

Amelia smiled up at her younger brother. "Not at all, Ken," she said. "Thank you for sparing us the details. This way," she added, with a mischievous twinkle in her eye, "I'll have a chance to brief Sandy on developments, too."

"Gossip, is it?" Ken harrumphed. But he gave Sandy and his sister a fond, warm look, obviously pleased by the strong bond of friendship that had developed between them.

"You'll eventually find out what I'm telling her," Amelia teased. "You just go on about your business and we'll go on about ours."

From the look on her face, Sandy was already certain that Amelia's "briefing" would prove to be good news. As soon as Ken and Fitz began strolling down the narrow street, Amelia confirmed Sandy's intuition by reaching into her pocket and pulling out a small tissue-wrapped object.

"Look," she whispered, unfolding the wrapping paper. On the palm of her hand rested a twinkling diamond ring.

Immediately Sandy leaned over and hugged her friend. "Oh, Amelia, I'm so happy for you," she said. "The Captain's proposed, hasn't he?"

Something was wrong, Sandy could tell. Amelia was smiling all right, but there was something tentative, even wan, about the expression on her noble face.

"You're the only one I've told," Amelia said. "Thomas McCabe is such a fine man, and we've grown so close in such a short time..."

"Didn't you accept his proposal?" Sandy said. "What about the ring?"

Amelia sighed. "I told him I had to think it over. He's such a dear man, he insisted I keep the ring until I decided. He's kept it with him always—it was in the ship's safe. It's been in his family for generations. He says if he could see me with it on my finger he'd know that I'd be with him always, too." She looked down at the sparkling diamond in her palm and added reflectively, "But I don't know if I can."

"But why?" Sandy wanted to know. "Don't you love him?"

"No, no," the older woman said hurriedly, "it's not that. I *do* love him—without a single doubt. That's what makes it so hard."

"You love him," Sandy repeated, pondering the mystery of her friend's words, "and *that* is what makes it so hard?"

Amelia sighed and looked down again at the ring in her hand, but she said nothing.

Puzzled, Sandy took her gaze away from her friend and looked all around, as if she could find a clue to the mystery of Amelia's hesitancy somewhere in their immediate environment.

There was the turbaned Indian—probably the restaurant owner Amelia had spoken about before—bringing more food to the Hartmanns' table. Mr. Hartmann was still glaring suspiciously in her direction, while whispering something to his wife, who nodded in silent agreement as she pushed another piece of marinated fish into her mouth.

Outside on the street Ken and Kenneally walked by, deep in conversation, paying no attention to the bustling shops or the open-air stalls in which the merchants displayed their many wares. How dignified and handsome Ken looked, Sandy thought, his hands clasped behind his back, listening as his aide whispered in his ear. As they passed the restaurant, Ken turned his head slightly and flashed Sandy a smile of such brilliance that it was all she could do to keep from jumping up and running to him. How she loved the man, and how much she wanted to kiss him right then!

Still nodding attentively as Kenneally spoke, Ken winked and blew Sandy a kiss. She smiled back at him, raised her hand to return the tender gesture, and stopped. Hartmann was looking, she knew, and she didn't want to give the gossips any more ammunition than they already had.

She could tell Ken was puzzled by her aborted gesture, but he and Kenneally kept walking and talking. Sandy hoped Ken didn't misunderstand, that he realized she was only prevented by propriety's sake from showing her affection.

Propriety's sake, Sandy repeated to herself. *That* was it!

"Amelia, *I* know what's wrong," Sandy said urgently. "I know why you're hesitating about accepting the ring of the man you love."

"You do?" Amelia asked excitedly. "Good, I'm glad *one* of us does."

"It's so perfect that you confided in me. I'm probably the only one in this whole cruise who would understand."

"Well, tell me, girl, don't keep me in suspense!"

"You're happy, aren't you, with Captain McCabe, happier than you've been in a long, long time?"

Amelia nodded in agreement.

"That's the problem!"

"What is?"

Sandy laughed. "Amelia, my dear friend, forgive me for saying this, but you're overcome by guilt at this happiness of yours." To herself she added, *It's the same problem I've been having myself, only in my case...* Sandy nodded in Mr. Hartmann's direction, letting the words trail off. She could see that Amelia—not one to be in the dark for long—had already grasped her meaning.

"Oh, Sandy, you *do* love Ken! You know, I've felt from the beginning that you were somehow right for each other." Leaning over to whisper her next words, Amelia went on, "In your case, any guilt feelings you may have are compounded by all the Hartmanns and Babs Tellers of this world trying to *make* you feel guilty because you've found a new love. Lord knows it's bad enough in *my* case, being widowed for less than a year, thinking I'd never find anyone after losing Marshall. You're absolutely right, dear, *dear* Sandy. How can I thank you for this? I've felt disloyal to my late husband's memory when the truth of the matter is that Marshall would be the first to want my happiness. Isn't that so?"

"Yes, *yes*," Sandy said, "a thousand times yes!" She knew that the same oppressive guilt feelings that had shackled Amelia were at the root of much of her own trouble too. She could tell that her insight was freeing Amelia of her unnecessary burden and it was doing the same for her. Tears welled in Sandy's eyes as she saw her friend slip the engagement ring on her finger.

"Thank you," Amelia whispered. "Thank you for helping me see."

Sandy wanted to hug her friend, to tell her that through her she, too, had just come to see the truth. But at the very instant that she was smiling all misty-eyed at Amelia, she noticed that, on the other side of the restaurant, Mr. Hartmann was slapping his wife on the back. He was offering her a glass of water, but she waved frantically and pushed it from his hand.

To Sandy's horror, she saw that Mrs. Hartmann was trying to speak but no words were coming out. Within seconds, the look on Mr. Hartmann's face changed from irritability to concern to panic—his wife was turning blue!

The Secret Service and the Executive Protective Agency had trained Sandy well for many contingencies. She knew just what was wrong and exactly what to do.

Without even taking a second to respond to Amelia's startled exclamation, Sandy jumped up from the table so quickly that she knocked a plate of food from a passing waiter's hand. Heedless of the staring patrons, she dashed across the restaurant and over to the frantic woman. Ignoring a panic-stricken Mr. Hartmann, who shouted at Sandy to keep away, Sandy looked directly into Mrs. Hartmann's frightened, bulging eyes and asked her as calmly as possible, "Are you choking, Mrs. Hartmann? Nod your head if you can't speak."

Mrs. Hartmann's head bobbed up and down furiously. Her mouth was open wide as she tried to gasp for air.

"Don't worry," Sandy said in that same level tone. "I'm going to help you."

In his concern and panic, Mr. Hartmann tried to push her away. "Get away, you—you . . ." he sputtered, as his wife lurched to her feet, knocking her chair back and clawing the air with her hands. The commotion drew all eyes in the restaurant to the scene. Finally, the other patrons were realizing that an emergency was in progress.

"Call an ambulance," a voice yelled.

Someone else screamed at the sight of Mrs. Hartmann, gasping and choking and flailing all around her.

Sandy ignored it all. Deftly, she side-stepped Mr. Hartmann's extended arm. In one neat motion she slipped behind the choking woman and kicked the upended chair out of her way.

Mr. Hartmann was screaming incoherently in her ear, but still Sandy paid him no attention. She reached around Mrs. Hartmann's ample waist as if she intended to hug her from behind. She positioned one fist just below Mrs.

Hartmann's rib cage. She covered the fist with the hand reaching from the other side.

"Relax," she whispered into Mrs. Hartmann's ear. At the same time, with all her strength, she squeezed her arms together, hugging Mrs. Hartmann as hard as she could, driving her fist quickly and forcefully into the woman's abdomen.

"Aah!" Mrs. Hartmann exclaimed. A chunk of food flew out of her mouth. She took several quick, ragged breaths and fell into her husband's arms. The deadly obstruction—a piece of fish—was lying on the floor.

And suddenly all was pandemonium! The restaurant patrons broke into spontaneous applause. The owner was at the elbow of Mr. Hartmann, apologizing and disclaiming responsibility at the same time, while offering to drive Mrs. Hartmann to the hospital himself. Mr. Hartmann, one arm around his wife, was refusing all assistance and adamantly insisting that only the ship's doctor was qualified to examine his wife. Mrs. Hartmann, color returning to her face, was saying to everyone in sight that she was just fine now, that there was no reason to be upset.

Amelia had rushed to Sandy's side, and Ken and Kenneally were watching from the street. The restaurant's Indian owner, his turban slightly askew, came up to her and said in a sibilant English accent, "I believe you have just saved that woman's life. Of course, there will be no charge for the meal."

12

It was sunset and the *Voyager Queen* was sailing out of Suva harbor. Sandy was standing at the stern rail on the Promenade Deck watching the sharp mountain peaks of the Tamavua Heights recede into the purple distance as the ship made its majestic way into the open sea. She had on a blue and white striped silk dress, one of her favorite new acquisitions. Her blond hair blew freely in the evening breeze.

She was thinking about Fiji and all that had happened. She knew that Amelia would be with the Captain tonight and that Ken would soon join her on deck and that together they would go to dinner. She remembered how wonderful their love-making had been—the touch of his hands, the hardness of his body, the way he made her feel . . . Her reverie was broken by the sound of someone behind her clearing his throat.

"Ma'am," Mr. Hartmann said, stepping up to the railing next to her. "I don't quite know how to thank you for what happened today."

Still looking out at the darkening distant peaks, Sandy shrugged. "There's no need, Mr. Hartmann. The Heimlich Maneuver is standard procedure for choking prevention. You'd be surprised how common an occurrence it is."

"Well, ma'am, it may be all in a day's work to you, but I am truly grateful. I spoke to the ship's doctor, told him what you did, and he said I was damn lucky you were around. He said I could have lost my dear girl today."

Again, Sandy shrugged. "It's part of my job," she said.

"Ma'am, that was quick thinking and fast action in that restaurant," Mr. Hartmann replied. "You're one hell of a bodyguard. And that Senator fellow must be a lot smarter than I gave him credit for to find a pretty little lady with your qualifications to watch over him. I just want to say . . . I just want to say . . ."

"It's really not necessary, Mr. Hartmann," Sandy said softly, turning to the tongue-tied Texan. "What you've just said is thanks enough."

Without looking at her, Mr. Hartmann reached into the pocket of his western jacket and pulled out a small yellow cylinder, which he placed in Sandy's hand.

"I was terrible toward you and your man," he whispered. "I let that Babs Teller woman convince me it was all some big joke, just a prank we were playing on you. No one's seen the pictures. I haven't even developed the negatives yet. I'm sorry. If you're ever in Texas, come to our store and pick out anything you want. Price is no object, y'hear." And with that, Mr. Hartmann rushed away.

Sandy was still looking at the roll of film in her hand when Ken appeared at her side. As always, he was the essence of elegance in his tuxedo.

"I saw you speaking with your new friend," he said casually, "so I waited until Mr. Hartmann was finished."

Sandy held out the roll of film in her palm. "We don't have to worry about blackmail anymore, or having our picture on the seven o'clock news."

"That's good," Ken said coolly, without the sense of relief in his voice that Sandy expected.

She matched her tone to his cool calmness. "Would you like this as a memento?" she asked, offering him the film. "Or perhaps for your next campaign biography.

You could appeal to the lechery vote," she added with more sarcasm than she'd intended.

Ken laughed. "I guess I have that constituency already. That's the problem, as Kenneally never tires of telling me. No, I had in mind burial at sea for this film."

She handed the roll to him. "Go ahead, then no one can hurt us."

With a quick snap of the wrist, he pitched the roll of film over the side, letting it fall into the inky ocean far below. "Gone forever," he said, putting his arm around Sandy's waist. "Hungry?" he asked.

"Not really," she replied.

"Good," Ken said avidly. "I was hoping you weren't. Let's go back up to your stateroom. For once, nobody is going to bother us for a good long while."

Ken gave her waist a squeeze of endearment and leaned down to kiss the lobe of her ear. "I could use the services of a good bodyguard," he whispered.

Sandy smiled up at him despite herself. She still had questions, but his closeness and his touch pushed them out of her mind.

In truth, she realized as they walked back along the deserted deck, to be so close to him was all she wanted. The hell with all the tomorrows!

She awakened the following morning feeling the warm glow that only comes after a night of exquisitely satisfying lovemaking. She stretched voluptuously, rolled over, and reached out for Ken, but he was already gone.

Sandy showered, then slipped on a short-sleeved plaid dress of light linen with an above-the-knee hem and front buttons. Around her waist she fastened a narrow leather belt, and she stepped into a pair of soft leather sandals. Because she was feeling especially frisky, she left the top three as well as the bottom two wooden buttons unfastened.

She felt carefree and happy as she walked out into the

sitting room. She was idly combing her hair with her fingers and thinking about picking up the phone and having a big breakfast sent up when she saw the headline on the newspaper thrown carelessly onto the coffee table. At once her happiness vanished. She felt she must be cursed, but she wasn't one for fatalism, and the feeling quickly gave way to furious anger.

The newspaper was a cheap-looking Australian tabloid, one of a number of newspapers and news magazines transported most nights to the *Voyager Queen* by helicopter and delivered right to the cabin door of the passengers. Sandy had been too involved in her own troubles to read them, but this time the words screamed at her from the page. Dread mixed with rage and disgust as Sandy picked the tabloid up and read its shocking banner headline:

> *ISLAND PILOT TELLS ALL: 'I FLEW THE SENATOR AND HIS BLONDE BODYGUARD TO A NIGHT OF PAGAN PASSION!'*

The words swam before her eyes. Her lower lip trembled as she read the pilot's sordid description of the lovely Fijian idyl she and Ken had enjoyed. How soiled their afternoon and night of pleasure became in the pilot's base and degrading retelling! She couldn't stand to read more than a few words before she felt as if all the light and air had been sucked out of the sunny room.

Behind her the door opened and Sandy spun around, the newspaper crushed in her tight and angry fist. Ken came in, looking as happy as she herself had felt only a few moments before. His step was as light and jaunty as the navy blue polo shirt and white cotton trousers he was wearing. Oblivious to the stricken expression on her face, he marched over, put his hands on her shoulders, and kissed her heartily on the mouth.

"Well, here's another thing we won't have to worry

about," he announced happily. "I just heard the movie company's leaving the cruise in a couple of days, when we get to Sydney. And *that,* you'll be relieved to hear, means that Babs Teller will be going too. It seems the company's studio went bankrupt or had a management change or something. Whatever it was, the whole production is shutting down immediately. What a loss for the world of entertainment!"

He paused, giving her a questioning look. "Hey, I thought you'd be delighted to get rid of Babs. What's the matter? You look like you're going to cry."

Wordlessly Sandy stepped back and held the tabloid up between them. "See," she said accusingly, her voice quivering. "I told you this would happen."

"Oh, that," Ken said so casually that Sandy dropped the newspaper to the floor and just gaped at him in surprise. He shook his handsome head in wry amusement. "Well, you certainly were right on the money about *that.* That old pilot couldn't wait to tattle to the press."

"'Tattle to the press'?" Sandy repeated in astonishment. "Maybe *you* can survive your reputation as a womanizer, but I'm probably ruined. Don't you care at all? Don't you see that this is just as bad as having the Hartmann photo published, maybe worse? Don't you care about all the damage done by this...this..."

"Piece of trash?" he finished helpfully.

"That's too mild for this, much too mild," Sandy sputtered in rage. She couldn't believe her eyes or her ears. Was Ken Rexford actually tut-tutting this latest outrage? Could that be an amused smile on his face? Sophistication was one thing, but this was quite another. This was the obliviousness of the rich dilettante. This was just what Senator Ken Rexford's political enemies were always accusing him of—recklessness. This was just how they would expect him to act!

"I can't believe you're taking it like this," Sandy gasped.

"Oh, come on, Sandy. How do you want me to take it?" he asked, in a tone that seemed plainly to say, Wise up, girl!

"But, but . . ."

"Look, Sandy," he said in an infuriatingly even tone of voice, the same tone he might use to a five-year-old, "I'd really like to explain further to you, even though it should be obvious that getting upset will do no good whatsoever. If you can just hang on for a few more days, I think I can make everything clear to you. There are ways to redeem our reputations, yours and mine. Right this minute I've got an important meeting with Fitz and Harvey, an appointment with the radio room to send out some important cables. Can't you trust me, Sandy?"

"Trust you?" she repeated icily. "Give me one good reason why I should trust you."

"Oh, Sandy, darling, please . . ."

She couldn't believe he had the unmitigated nerve to sound exasperated with her! "How dare you!" she said in an Arctic whisper that would have frozen a blast furnace. "Don't you 'Sandy, darling,' me! I will *not* be patronized! I will *not* be treated like merely the latest in the long line of Senator Rexford's many conquests."

Even if I am, she thought to herself in horror. Suddenly she realized he wasn't upset because it was all true! She was merely the latest in his long line of conquests!

She thought for a second that she would run over and slap him, but instead she turned and dashed to her cabin door, determined that at least she would deny him the satisfaction of seeing her break down and cry.

She stood in the doorway of her stateroom a moment, shaking with anger, and Ken stepped toward her, his hand outstretched. "Sandy, please . . ."

But she was ashamed and enraged and far beyond words. What a little fool she must seem to be.

As she stepped tentatively toward him, Sandy screamed, "I told you so!" and slammed the door in his face.

"Sandy?"

She didn't answer his knock.

"Sandy, please."

She stood silently on the other side of the door, listening to the rapid tatoo of his knocking. Tears were running freely down her cheeks. For a moment there was silence.

"Sandy . . . the steward's just brought me a message. The radio operators are ready. I've really got to go. We'll talk when I can get back to you, okay? Okay, Sandy?"

She didn't say a word, and she didn't intend to either.

There was no doubt in her mind now. When they docked in Sydney, she would give up this assignment. She would call Foster Milner in Washington and tell him she could not go on as bodyguard to this decadent, insensitive, unfathomable, *impossible* man.

It was only after she heard Ken's departing footsteps and the sound of the sitting-room door close that she finally threw herself down on her bed and began to shake with sobs.

13

SANDY STAYED IN her cabin, and Ken remained in conference. Not even Amelia's latest and best news could cheer Sandy up.

"There's a minister on the passenger list," Amelia shouted through the closed door of Sandy's cabin. "We're pressing him into service tomorrow, and you're the Maid of Honor!"

"Wonderful," Sandy said with genuine feeling. She threw open the door, kissed her friend, then quickly shut the door again. "I'll be there," she shouted back, throwing herself on the bed again. "Tomorrow."

Sandy ignored everyone else—from the maid wanting to clean the cabin to Kenneally advising her that the Senator's business was continuing on into the evening. She stayed in her room with a do-not-disturb sign on the door, and she wept. Eventually, she cried herself to sleep. Even then, her dreams, of handsome men whose faces she could not see and unbearably beautiful tropical isles, were tinged with unhappiness and the sense that it would all be gone in the blink of an eye.

When Sandy finally awakened, she discovered to her surprise that she had not only slept through the night, but had also slept away the entire morning and a good part of the afternoon as well. The wedding was in less than an hour!

Quickly, she bathed and dressed in an emerald green suit of Thai silk with peace buttons, which seemed suitable for a wedding. Combing her blond hair and looking at herself in the full-length bathroom mirror on the back of the bathroom door, Sandy thought ruefully to herself:

Sandy O'Hara, one look at yourself and it should be obvious why someone like Ken Rexford can't take you any more seriously than as a night's plaything. You've let all the movie-star talk turn your head. Sure you have nice features and your body's in shape from all the working-out you give it, but, let's face it, with your all-American looks you're fated to be no better than the perpetual ingenue. You're just not the grand lady that someone like Senator Kenneth Rexford would make his consort . . . and you never will be!

She sighed and turned away from the mirror. The picture of Amelia with her dashing Captain McCabe crossed her mind, and she was glad that *someone* would get another chance at true happiness. Stepping out of the door of her cabin for the first time in nearly two days, she added to herself: *It will never happen to me!*

In the hall Sandy discovered a small pile of newspapers that had been left during the night. She stepped over them, not bothering to look at them. Probably some cruel prankster had left them there to torment her.

The ceremony was to take place outside, beside the swimming pool on the Riviera Deck's stern, where the largest number of people would be able to congregate. For a backdrop there would be the magnificent Sydney, Australia harbor, one of the most spectacular settings in the entire world. Sandy's first sight of the scene, as she rushed to take her place with the small wedding party, almost took her breath away.

The *Voyager Queen*, surrounded by tugs and yachts of every description, had paused in the center of the vast harbor. Passengers lined every square foot of deck space, and the crew were in their dress whites, giving the occasion a most festive air, appropriate for the *Queen*'s home port. Bunting was draped over the railings, and uniformed stewards passed among the assembled passengers with trays of champagne.

It was a beautiful, crystalline day. From her vantage point near the swimming pool, Sandy saw every detail of the harbor and the skyline of the city, the largest in the British Commonwealth outside of London itself. Sandy could see both luxurious high-rise apartments and quaint nineteenth-century seaside villages. Dominating the harbor were Sydney's two great man-made attractions—the futuristic Opera House, its roofs resembling ships under full sail, and the Harbor Bridge, its single arch spanning the entire harbor like some great metal rainbow. It was an awe-inspiring vista, the ideal backdrop for a wedding.

Everyone Sandy knew on board was gathered around the swimming pool, from Babs Teller, who was furiously scribbling notes, to Miles, Rose, and the rest of the movie company and all Ken's aides. Ken, as best man, was there, too, wearing a dark suit with a white carnation in his lapel. Sandy had to admit how splendid he looked, telling herself at virtually the same instant not to care. For once, in keeping with the occasion, everyone, even Babs Teller, was smiling and looking benevolent.

Just before the brief ceremony began, Ken strolled over to Sandy. "It's not too late to make it a double wedding," he said, smiling.

His casualness absolutely infuriated her, and she began to turn away. "Hey, is that any way for the Maid of Honor to treat the Best Man?" he said, grabbing her arm before she could get away.

She smiled up at him, but under her breath she hissed, "Don't you realize everyone's here? Don't you see Babs Teller over there making notes on everything?"

"Who cares?" he responded expansively, confirming her worst fears. "Do you think anyone *really* believes what she writes? Besides," he added, "there are more important things in the newspapers these days, don't you agree?"

"I don't even know what you're talking about," Sandy told him, pulling her arm out of his grasp. "I have no interest in reading these scandal sheets." She started to walk away.

"Hey, Sandy," he called after her. "What about your job? You're supposed to be my bodyguard, remember? I *need* a bodyguard."

Infuriated by his cavalier attitude, Sandy spun around. "Why?" she retorted, heedless of who might overhear. "I'm the only one on this ship who might do you any damage!" Then she stalked off to the little alcove nearby, where Amelia was waiting for the ceremony to begin.

Dressed in a coral-silk, floor-length gown, Amelia was pacing the alcove nervously. "Do I look all right? Is everything going smoothly?"

"You look absolutely beautiful," Sandy assured her with a smile.

"And so do you," Amelia replied, picking a small white flower up from a table nearby. She walked over to Sandy and pinned the flower in Sandy's hair. "There," she said with some satisfaction. "It's an old family tradition. Everyone in the wedding party has on something white."

"Fine with me," Sandy told her, laughing affectionately.

"Are you *sure* everything's okay?" Amelia asked again.

"Amelia, you're a typical nervous bride," Sandy replied affectionately. "Everyone's just as friendly and happy as could be. Even your brother has decided to be charming to me."

Amelia was obviously only too glad to be distracted from her own jitters. She put her hands on Sandy's shoulder and looked her straight in the eye. "Sandy O'Hara," she said, "a couple of days ago you gave me some good advice—advice that saved my life as surely as you saved the life of that woman when she was choking. Now, I'm going to do you a favor and I'm going to give that advice right back to you. Don't let your worries and your guilt feelings get in the way of *your* happiness. That boy you once married would want your happiness, wouldn't he?"

"Yes, but—"

"No, buts," Amelia said sternly. "I know what you're going to say. You're all embarrassed by the scandal and the publicity and worried because my brother doesn't take it as hard as you do. Well, dear, a little bad publicity isn't the end of the world, and maybe you should take the trouble to find out why a man like my brother isn't concerned. After all, hasn't more than one columnist called him 'The Zorro of Modern Politics'? And you know what that means, don't you?"

"Well, I . . ."

"It means," Amelia explained in no uncertain terms, "that there's a lot more to my brother than meets the eye. He's using this playboy reputation of his for his own ends. He's playing it to the hilt for very good reasons."

"But still . . ."

From outside, the first organ chords of the ceremony sounded. "No buts," Amelia insisted. "I'm telling you to do the same thing you told me to do. Listen to your heart, Sandy!"

Shivers of joy went up and down Sandy's spine. Amelia was right *and* she was giving her approval to Sandy's love for her brother.

The brief shipboard ceremony went by in a blur for Sandy. All she knew was that Ken was standing next to her beaming at her and at his sister, and that Amelia's final words were whirling around and around in her mind. *Perhaps,* she thought to herself, *perhaps . . .*

Soon the "I dos" were said and the minister pronounced Thomas McCabe and Amelia Rexford Winston man and wife. When the Captain took his bride in his arms and kissed her, a great "Huzzah!" went up from the assembled crew, and all the passengers cheered and toasted the happy couple. As she and her husband marched down the poolside aisle, Amelia threw her bouquet of flowers directly into Sandy's hands.

Embarrassed, Sandy turned around with the bouquet in her hands, expecting to see at least a warm smile on Ken's face. But she was disappointed to find that he was listening intently as Kenneally whispered into his ear, and that he immediately left with his chief aide. As the crowd of crew and passengers began to mill around, heading gradually for one of the many receptions and parties planned for every deck of the ship, Sandy decided to go back to her cabin. She told herself she would return later to wish the newlyweds well. But for the moment she knew that, with Ken gone, she had no real reason to celebrate.

14

How could she have failed to see that, among the newspapers outside her door, there was a cablegram?

Quickly she tore it open and read the terse message: *ARRIVING SYDNEY 19th. STOP. E.T.A. THE QUEEN 4. P.M. STOP. FOSTER,* the message was signed.

Sandy was aghast at the message from her former boss at the Service. Today *was* the 19th, she realized. In a rising panic she glanced down at the clock on the night table next to her bed. It was 4:10 P.M. already! That meant he could be aboard at that very moment, and how would it look if she wasn't on deck to greet him!

Sandy went running out of the stateroom. Soon she was back out on deck, peering anxiously over the side. She realized that he must be coming for no other reason than to relieve her of her post, that word of the scandal had reached him in Washington and he felt he had no other choice. Well, she would save him the trouble and offer him her resignation before he could say a word.

Still, she would not give him the satisfaction of finding her hiding in her room. She would be there on the upper deck to greet him—assuming he wasn't on board somewhere already—and report like the professional that she was.

Oh, please, please don't cry, she said to herself, looking all around. A steady stream of passengers and visitors were coming and going from the pier where the ship had berthed as soon as the wedding ceremony was ended, but there was no sign of Foster Milner, the man who had trusted her to handle this assignment in the first place. Having let him down hurt as much as anything.

There went the movie company, filing off the ship, their battered trunks in tow. Babs Teller and the movie director himself were at the head of the line of departing actors and technicians. The columnist, Sandy realized, was waving in her direction.

"Bye, honey," she called to her with sincerity in her voice, as if they were old friends. "Give my best wishes to the dear Senator."

Sandy waved back tentatively and managed a small smile, even though she was amazed at the gossip columnist's temerity. First she destroys my reputation, she thought with amazement, and costs me my career, and now she acts as if she's my best friend!

Miles and Rose were leaving too. Sandy wasn't surprised when Miles waved goodbye, but she was definitely taken aback when Rose joined him. They were both waving something in their hands, and they seemed awfully happy for two people who had just had their movie jerked out from under them in mid-production. They must be better actors than she had realized, Sandy thought, returning their waves and straining to hear what Miles was shouting.

". . . contract!" he shouted, pointing to the paper in his hand. "Co-leads in an Australian TV mini-series," he added, pointing to Rose and himself.

Rose cupped a hand around her lips and yelled up, "The publicity did it! We wouldn't have gotten it without all this publicity!"

Sandy was astounded by this development, but she just shouted back her congratulations and waved to the departing actors. How well everything was working out for everybody—except for her, she thought with resignation, still searching the crowds for some sign of her boss.

What she saw then almost made her rub her eyes in disbelief.

At the center of a protective group of huge men, all wearing sunglasses and tight-fitting suits, was a pair of tall, exotic-looking bearded men, both dressed in the flowing white burnoose so unmistakably the sign of the strife-torn island of Mauristan and by now so familiar to Sandy.

The taller of the two men was dressed in a burnoose trimmed in red and gold. The other had a blue band around his hood. Sandy paused next to a group of passengers long enough to hear someone say, ". . . the leaders of north and south Mauristan . . . !"

Although she hadn't been following the crisis since she had left Washington, since she'd been avoiding the newspapers and their gossip, Sandy knew they had to be the central figures in the war that had been occupying the attention of Washington for months. What on earth were they doing here, in Sydney, Australia, together, in apparent harmony, preparing to board the *Voyager Queen?*

What Sandy saw next she really could not believe. Walking just behind the two regal Mauristanians was none other than Foster Milner himself! And there, sweeping along with a flying wedge of burnoose-clad bodyguards, was another familiar face—Gus Flowers, her partner in the martial-arts demonstrations she had spent the last year giving around Washington!

Sandy watched in amazement as the group made its way onto the ship. Electronic strobes flashed and questions flew from the advancing party of men, who seemed to represent the entire Australian press corps, and those of the rest of the world as well. Whatever was going on, the press was obviously being welcomed this time.

When the group had passed her, Sandy turned and hurriedly took a shortcut she had discovered to the elevators on A-Deck, from which she knew instinctively they would emerge. She was still in a daze a few minutes later when the entire group swept out of the arriving elevators and marched directly to the Senator's suite at the end of the hall.

The rulers of Mauristan and their little troop of guards didn't pause or even miss a step as they passed Sandy. Foster nodded solemnly at her as he walked briskly by. "Good job," he said out of the side of his mouth.

Gus gave her the thumbs-up sign and a big smile as he passed with the other guards, but he didn't stop or say anything.

As Sandy watched, the entire group arrived at Ken's stateroom door. Foster knocked briskly, and the door was opened by Kenneally. For a second Ken was framed in the open doorway and he and the two burnoose-clad men embraced in warm greeting. Then they and Foster were ushered inside and Kenneally slammed the door shut behind them.

Sandy was agog. She watched as her old partner Gus posted his phalanx of bodyguards all around the entrance to the stateroom, and the security force from Mauristan scattered itself in between them. Then, finally, he came over to her, bent his battered boxer's head down to her, and gave her a warm kiss on the cheek.

"Great t'see ya, kid," he croaked. "You've done one hell of a job. Everybody's talking about it."

"I'll bet," Sandy replied tonelessly, all too aware of how the scandal would have been received on the Washington cocktail-party circuit.

Gus apparently did not hear her response as he added, "Everybody thinks that tropical romance stuff was the perfect cover."

"What?!" Sandy blurted.

"Hell, yes, kid. Even that gossip columnist, the one who started the whole thing."

"Babs Teller?"

"Yeah, I think that's her name. She just wrote a big

story about how she was in on the whole thing, admitting that she just made up all those stories about you and the Senator to assist her government. Don't you get the papers here, kid?"

A vision of the stack of papers outside her stateroom door came before Sandy's eyes. "Well," she said, "I haven't been reading them recently, Gus. Why don't you just tell me what you and Foster Milner and half of Mauristan and . . . all these people are doing here?"

"You're not kidding, are you, kid? You really don't know?"

"Look, Gus, ever since Hawaii I've known this trip involved something important, but that's all I know."

She stepped back to let two huge television cameras roll past her as the press kept arriving, positioning themselves with cameras and microphones in the hallway around Ken's closed stateroom door.

Something very big was happening, right there on the *Voyager Queen*. Something very big, and Ken Rexford was somehow at the center of it.

"Gus, tell me," Sandy whispered, stepping back to his side.

Gus laughed and squeezed her shoulder. Lowering his voice, he began, "They really didn't tell you about any of this . . . about the Senator's role in bringing the Mauristan war to an end? Peace, Sandy. That's what this is all about. At this very moment, behind that door, the two factions in Mauristan's civil war are signing a peace agreement. That's why Milner and I are here. We've worked behind the scenes with Senator Rexford on this for months. It's our reward, being on hand for the big moment. The little war that's had the Russians and the U.S. growling at each other is over, and the Senator's accomplished it, practically singlehandedly."

Sandy stared up at Gus. "This trip, the meetings in Hawaii, Fiji?"

Gus nodded. "Sure. The Mauristan Assistance Group

met him in both places. His family's oil company, you know, Worldwide Oil, has volunteered to lease equipment and send training teams to Mauristan so the oil under the island is drilled properly. The U.N. has set up a committee to see that the spoils are divided equally between north and south Mauristan. That means, too, that Russia and the USA will get to buy equal shares and the income will be shared by both factions on the island."

"That's . . . that's absolutely amazing!" Sandy gasped. "Has Russia really agreed to this?"

"They've had to. They were outvoted in the U.N. yesterday. All other parties agreed. The Mauristanians have stopped their fighting. They'll allow Worldwide Oil to assist operations. You see, Sandy, this is the real reason Senator Rexford dropped out of the Senate race last summer. He thought his connections could bring this crisis to an end, but he couldn't float around having clandestine meetings if he were in office. He could never have kept the press at bay. I'd say he's real presidential timber now!"

Sandy consciously closed her mouth. Her jaw had dropped open in astonishment at all that Gus was telling her.

But Gus was looking at her in amazement too. "You mean they really didn't tell you anything? How typical. Milner's bureaucrats probably figured the bodyguard had no *need* to know."

Sandy just shook her head back and forth. "Figures, doesn't it?"

"Well, you may not have known what you were up against, but you did quite a job. We heard about Honolulu harbor and Suva, about those skirmishes. The would-be assassin you stopped? Turned out he was some well-to-do businessman from the northern part of the island hoping to drill Mauristan's oil himself. He thought Worldwide Oil was after it. He just flipped out, I guess."

Gus paused, and a twinkle came to his eyes. "The

...then those first stories were true?" he whispered. "You and the Senator on the tropical island...I mean, you really, you and he are...?"

"Doubtful, Gus," Sandy interrupted. Her amazement at Ken's political victory now gave way to sudden anger...or maybe it was grief?

Gus looked perplexed as he said in a gravelly whisper, "Well anyway, you'll certainly get a commendation out of this, kid," and, kissing her gently on the forehead, he stepped over to join his men. "See you later, Sandy," he said, giving her a wave.

Sandy's heart was tumbling with emotion. Now, at last, she knew the truth. That was why Ken had made love to her, allowed Babs Teller to give the world the stories that made him seem the great lover of all time. He had *tried*, in fact, to expose their romance to the press, all to cover up the real reasons for his trip, what he was really up to. Not letting her in on the truth of his mission, Ken had set her up to play perfectly into his hands. She had been the perfect mask—innocent, naive, vulnerable...

Now he was basking in glory. Maybe Sandy did deserve that commendation. After all, hadn't she compromised herself, been lured into Ken's arms, all to help her government out?

Suddenly Ken's door opened. There was a great flutter of excitement among the press. With the two leaders of Mauristan on either side of him, Ken stepped into the doorway. The three posed for pictures, the burnoose-clad men taking turns shaking Ken's hand and then grasping each other's. Now Ken was answering the questions of some of the television reporters who held microphones up to him.

Sandy didn't listen. Anger and resentment were pounding through her. But she couldn't escape yet. She saw Foster Milner making his way toward her from behind the crush around Ken. If Gus was right, he wasn't coming to fire her after all. Then she would have to offer him her resignation.

"Sandy O'Hara," her former boss said affectionately as he took her hands in his. "You've done us proud. If it weren't for you, I don't know if the Senator could have accomplished all this. Now he deserves a real rest for the remainder of the cruise. And you too, my dear. I want you to take it as paid vacation and we'll start your career up again when you get back. I've already talked with your Agency. I've asked Gus to stay on board as the Senator's working bodyguard."

There wasn't a thing Sandy could say except, "Thank you, Foster. Thank you."

"Congratulations, Sandy." He pressed her hands warmly and turned abruptly to give his attention to the goings on.

Sandy couldn't take any more. She made her way out of the crowded hall, around the corner to her own stateroom. There, in front of her door, was the stack of unread newspapers she had been ignoring. Babs Teller's latest story, news of peace on Mauristan, news of Ken . . . probably all there in black and white.

Somehow, even now, she didn't want to see it all in print—her name linked with Ken's, when it never really could be, all the praise for him. Sandy was weary of the whole subject.

She loaded the papers in her arms and unlocked the door, letting it fall back, unlatched. Dumping the papers in a pile on her bed, she sat down next to them and stared at the wall. What was she going to do now? Spend two more months near this man who had used her to his own ends, for all the world to see? What need did he have of her now? Gus would provide protection; Ken didn't even need her as a decoy for the press anymore.

Suddenly Ken himself burst through her unlocked door.

15

"YES? SANDY SAID COLDLY, looking up at him with a start. "It didn't look as though you needed me out there. There were plenty of bodyguards."

Ken was standing next to her, looking down into her eyes.

"Those papers," he said. "You haven't read any of those, have you?" he asked her softly.

"No," she said, looking down at them. "I didn't want to read about myself as 'the blonde bombshell.' But I guess I missed a little world news as well."

"I told you I would tell you what was going on when I could." Ken's tone was surprisingly gentle and almost caring as he moved toward where she was sitting. "It was important that no one on this ship have any idea what I was doing, except Fitz and Harvey, of course. No one was to know what my meetings were about, Sandy, or to get a hint of what I was trying to do."

"Not even your own bodyguard?" she asked sharply.

"Not even you. Not even Amelia, who *sensed* a few things. I hadn't told her why I was really taking this trip. These negotiations only succeeded because they took place off the beaten track, far from the events themselves, and far from the eagle eyes of the press . . . for the most part."

"Oh, no!" she said. "No. The press didn't catch on to your meetings? *I* gave them something to write about instead. You took me off into the jungles, made love to me so there'd be something else to make headlines in

the gossip columns! That helped throw them off the track,
didn't it!"

Ken sat down next to her on the bed. He put his hand
on her shoulder. "Sandy, listen to me. This is what happened. Letting the press think this was all a big tryst was
Harvey's idea. When he saw us from the helicopter, he
wasn't even sure it was you and me down there. But it
gave him the idea. You see, in Honolulu one reporter
from a major wire service had gotten wind of the attempt
on my life at the memorial. Harvey told him he'd give
him a hot bit of gossip if he would keep the lid on that
story. And it worked. The press decided my big interest
on this trip was *you.*"

"Then you traded my reputation for your political
victory. Isn't that what it amounts to?" she hissed at him.

"I would never have made that choice, Sandy. But
Harvey did it on his own. Once Babs Teller realized that
we were a hot story, I'm afraid it was too late to do
anything to protect your reputation anyway. After that,
things were heating up. Cables and calls to and from this
ship. The meetings on Fiji. I'll admit the stories about
you and me did seem a lucky decoy for what was really
going on, and occasionally I was even helping to give
the impression. But I thought that, well, very soon, it
wouldn't matter anyway."

"Wouldn't matter?" Sandy was aghast. Did he mean
now that he didn't need her anymore it no longer mattered
to him what reputation she took away with her?

"If you haven't read these papers, then I guess you
didn't get my messages."

"Messages?" she repeated questioningly.

Ken reached down, picked up the bottom newspaper,
and gave it a vigorous shake. Several handwritten notes
fluttered out from between the papers. "Here," he said
simply, handing them to her.

But Sandy had another question. "But this latest Babs

Teller stuff," she began. "She wasn't *really* in on all this, was she? Did she know she was helping divert attention from your negotiations?"

"Of course not." Ken chuckled. "She's just making sure she doesn't look too silly, now that the world knows what I was really doing. I'm really sorry, Sandy, that you were the last to know, that your feelings have been hurt by this. I didn't plan it this way . . . just as I didn't plan on falling in love with you, even though Kenneally's been lobbying me to ask you to marry me for days. He says it's just the thing I need to take care of my image problems once and for all."

"Love?" Sandy repeated. "Marriage?"

"Look at my notes to you. Read them," he demanded. "Read them now."

They all said the same thing: *"Marry me! Marry me! Please, Sandy darling, marry me!"*

"Of course, I'm asking you *despite* the fact that it's good politics," he said wryly, reaching over to help her rise to her feet with him.

She let him put his arm around her and lead her to the terrace window overlooking the bow of the ship and the picturesque harbor.

Incongruously, she found herself asking yet another question. "The hotels you were talking about, in Hawaii and Fiji, were those just decoys too?"

"No." Ken smiled. "We really are going to build the hotels someday. But we'll do studies and careful planning to be sure we don't disrupt local life. We'll have to make many more visits, you and I, before all the decisions can be made."

He leaned over to kiss her, gently at first, then more insistently, and Sandy felt herself melting into him, her body warming to his. But she pulled away and looked into his dark, intelligent eyes, which even she could see now were brimming with love for her.

"But I have one more question, Ken. The first time we met, in the closet," she smiled, "why did you kiss me?"

A broad smile swept across his handsome face as he guided her back toward the bed. "That," he said, "was the wisest, absolutely most spontaneous, irrational bit of behavior I can lay claim to. There I was, not only safely avoiding the panting press, but suddenly close to the beautiful woman wearing an old green warmup suit that, I guess, I had just fallen in love with a few minutes before under the rotunda of the Capitol building."

"You had? I mean, right then, that minute?"

"Seems so, in retrospect anyway." His eyes were so wide and bright that she could see herself reflected in them. "I must have been thinking to myself that day— 'In the proper attire, that young woman would make an exemplary First Lady of the United States.' And that was even before I knew you were a first rate bodyguard. And I'll really need protection if I do get as far as the White House, you know." His expression was playful, loving, challenging.

Sandy reached out and pushed him gently backwards until he fell willingly, loosely into the pile of still-rolled newspapers on the bed. She scooped up the nearest ones and dumped them on his head. Ken pretended to flail in distress, saying in between the thuds, "But you haven't answered me, Sandy! Will you accept my proposal? Will you make me the happiest man on earth? Will you?"

Sandy fell next to him on the bed, her head pillowed on newspapers. They faced each other, nose to nose. A big smile was on Sandy's lips, and she knew that her happiness was reflected in her eyes. But she still didn't speak.

"Well, Ms. Bodyguard? We still have two months left on the *Queen* and half the world to see on our honeymoon. What do you say?"

"As if you needed to sweeten the proposal," she murmured before his lips found hers.

As she melted into his embrace, Sandy knew that their real voyage together was just beginning.

**WATCH FOR
6 NEW TITLES EVERY MONTH!**

Second Chance at Love

_____ 06195-6 **SHAMROCK SEASON #35** Jennifer Rose
_____ 06304-5 **HOLD FAST TIL MORNING #36** Beth Brookes
_____ 06282-0 **HEARTLAND #37** Lynn Fairfax
_____ 06408-4 **FROM THIS DAY FORWARD #38** Jolene Adams
_____ 05968-4 **THE WIDOW OF BATH #39** Anne Devon
_____ 06400-9 **CACTUS ROSE #40** Zandra Colt
_____ 06401-7 **PRIMITIVE SPLENDOR #41** Katherine Swinford
_____ 06424-6 **GARDEN OF SILVERY DELIGHTS #42** Sharon Francis
_____ 06521-8 **STRANGE POSSESSION #43** Johanna Phillips
_____ 06326-6 **CRESCENDO #44** Melinda Harris
_____ 05818-1 **INTRIGUING LADY #45** Daphne Woodward
_____ 06547-1 **RUNAWAY LOVE #46** Jasmine Craig
_____ 06423-8 **BITTERSWEET REVENGE #47** Kelly Adams
_____ 06541-2 **STARBURST #48** Tess Ewing
_____ 06540-4 **FROM THE TORRID PAST #49** Ann Cristy
_____ 06544-7 **RECKLESS LONGING #50** Daisy Logan
_____ 05851-3 **LOVE'S MASQUERADE #51** Lillian Marsh
_____ 06148-4 **THE STEELE HEART #52** Jocelyn Day
_____ 06422-X **UNTAMED DESIRE #53** Beth Brookes
_____ 06651-6 **VENUS RISING #54** Michelle Roland
_____ 06595-1 **SWEET VICTORY #55** Jena Hunt
_____ 06575-7 **TOO NEAR THE SUN #56** Aimée Duvall
_____ 05625-1 **MOURNING BRIDE #57** Lucia Curzon
_____ 06411-4 **THE GOLDEN TOUCH #58** Robin James
_____ 06596-X **EMBRACED BY DESTINY #59** Simone Hadary
_____ 06660-5 **TORN ASUNDER #60** Ann Cristy
_____ 06573-0 **MIRAGE #61** Margie Michaels
_____ 06650-8 **ON WINGS OF MAGIC #62** Susanna Collins

All of the above titles are $1.75 per copy

Available at your local bookstore or return this form to:

SECOND CHANCE AT LOVE
Book Mailing Service, P.O. Box 690, Rockville Cntr., NY 11570

Please send me the titles checked above. I enclose _____ .
Include 75¢ for postage and handling if one book is ordered; 50¢ per book for
two to five. If six or more are ordered, postage is free. California, Illinois, New
York and Tennessee residents please add sales tax.

NAME _____

ADDRESS _____

CITY_____ STATE/ZIP_____
Allow six weeks for delivery.   **SK-41**

_____ 05816-5 **DOUBLE DECEPTION** #63 Amanda Troy
_____ 06675-3 **APOLLO'S DREAM** #64 Claire Evans
_____ 06680-X **THE ROGUE'S LADY** #69 Anne Devon
_____ 06687-7 **FORSAKING ALL OTHERS** #76 LaVyrle Spencer
_____ 06689-3 **SWEETER THAN WINE** #78 Jena Hunt
_____ 06690-7 **SAVAGE EDEN** #79 Diane Crawford
_____ 06691-5 **STORMY REUNION** #80 Jasmine Craig
_____ 06692-3 **THE WAYWARD WIDOW** #81 Anne Mayfield
_____ 06693-1 **TARNISHED RAINBOW** #82 Jocelyn Day
_____ 06694-X **STARLIT SEDUCTION** #83 Anne Reed
_____ 06695-8 **LOVER IN BLUE** #84 Aimée Duvall
_____ 06696-6 **THE FAMILIAR TOUCH** #85 Lynn Lawrence
_____ 06697-4 **TWILIGHT EMBRACE** #86 Jennifer Rose
_____ 06698-2 **QUEEN OF HEARTS** #87 Lucia Curzon
_____ 06850-0 **PASSION'S SONG** #88 Johanna Phillips
_____ 06851-9 **A MAN'S PERSUASION** #89 Katherine Granger
_____ 06852-7 **FORBIDDEN RAPTURE** #90 Kate Nevins
_____ 06853-5 **THIS WILD HEART** #91 Margarett McKean
_____ 06854-3 **SPLENDID SAVAGE** #92 Zandra Colt
_____ 06855-1 **THE EARL'S FANCY** #93 Charlotte Hines
_____ 06858-6 **BREATHLESS DAWN** #94 Susanna Collins
_____ 06859-4 **SWEET SURRENDER** #95 Diana Mars
_____ 06860-8 **GUARDED MOMENTS** #96 Lynn Fairfax
_____ 06861-6 **ECSTASY RECLAIMED** #97 Brandy LaRue
_____ 06862-4 **THE WIND'S EMBRACE** #98 Melinda Harris
_____ 06863-2 **THE FORGOTTEN BRIDE** #99 Lillian Marsh

All of the above titles are $1.75 per copy

Available at your local bookstore or return this form to:

SECOND CHANCE AT LOVE
Book Mailing Service, P.O. Box 690, Rockville Cntr., NY 11570

Please send me the titles checked above. I enclose _____ .
Include 75¢ for postage and handling if one book is ordered; 50¢ per book for
two to five. If six or more are ordered, postage is free. California, Illinois, New
York and Tennessee residents please add sales tax.

NAME _____

ADDRESS _____

CITY_____ STATE/ZIP _____

Allow six weeks for delivery.   SK-41

WHAT READERS SAY ABOUT
SECOND CHANCE AT LOVE BOOKS

"Your books are the greatest!"
—*M. N., Carteret, New Jersey**

"I have been reading romance novels for quite some time, but the SECOND CHANCE AT LOVE books are the most enjoyable."
—*P. R., Vicksburg, Mississippi**

"I enjoy SECOND CHANCE [AT LOVE] more than any books that I have read and I do read a lot."
—*J. R., Gretna, Louisiana**

"For years I've had my subscription in to Harlequin. Currently there is a series called Circle of Love, but you have them all beat."
—*C. B., Chicago, Illinois**

"I really think your books are exceptional...I read Harlequin and Silhouette and although I still like them, I'll buy your books over theirs. SECOND CHANCE [AT LOVE] is more interesting and holds your attention and imagination with a better story line..."
—*J. W., Flagstaff, Arizona**

"I've read many romances, but yours take the 'cake'!"
—*D. H., Bloomsburg, Pennsylvania**

"Have waited ten years for *good* romance books. Now I have them."
—*M. P., Jacksonville, Florida**

*Names and addresses available upon request